D0984987

Thank You for Being Concerned and Sensitive

The

Iowa

Short

Fiction

Award

University of

Iowa Press

Iowa City

Jim Henry

Thank You for Being Concerned and Sensitive

University of Iowa Press, Iowa City 52242

Printed in the United States of America

 This is a work of fiction; any resemblance to actual events or persons is entirely coincidental.

Printed on acid-free paper

Library of Congress Cataloging-in-Publication Data

Henry, Jim, 1962–

Thank you for being concerned and sensitive / Jim Henry.

p. cm.—(The Iowa short fiction award)

ISBN 0-87745-610-0

I. Title. II. Series.

PS3558.E39765T48 1997

813'.54—dc21 97-17332

01 00 99 98 97 C 5 4 3 2 1

To the memory of Robert Burns Henry

When I was a child, it was the winters

that I hated the most. All the other children

had little red sleds. Mine was beige.

That's when I first noticed the pains.

JACK DOUGLAS, *My Brother Was an Only Child*

Contents

ACKNOWLEDGMENTS

The author would like to express his gratitude to a few others who continually supported him over the years. These people include his patient and endlessly generous mother, Daniel Keyes, Mark Mirsky, Deborah Garrison, Abby Warren, Cindy Washabaugh, Martha Conway, Neal Chandler, and, especially, Sheila Schwartz.

The following stories in this collection appeared, in slightly different form, in these publications: "Motherhurt" in *Studies in Contemporary Satire* and "Observer Status" in *Whiskey Island*.

Thank You for Being Concerned and Sensitive

Motherhurt

Mother's been hurt somehow, that much is clear. Paul is over in the corner chanting. He is trying to drown us out. He's read some book, some book about chanting. He says he will be different. He won't let us ruin him. All we can really do is nod. Paul is like that. Father is pacing, a frantic look across his reddened face. Mother's been hurt, it is her we must deal with now. The crisis of the moment is hers, Paul's self-indulgent chanting notwithstanding.

We break into little groups to discuss courses of action. I end up with Father and Timmy and Jonas and Sylvia and Paul. The six of us decide to open up a bag of chips. Thomas and Fred and Lila and Billy and Steve form another group and we hear them bickering over points of order. The last group is Baby, Scotty, and Phil. They're the three youngest and they don't really constitute a group but we let them pretend because if you don't let children pretend they grow up doing surprising, frightening things that, really, can be quite horrifying. This has been documented extensively by doctors and clinicians and the like. It's not just something I've conveniently made up as some in this family might have you believe.

Father passes the chips around and belches quietly. He is gruff, overbearing, at times flatulent. We all love him dearly. He is like a little boy lost in a hellishly frightening spook house. As are we all. "Your mother is a very sensitive woman," he tells us, although this we already know.

"What do you think it is?" Sylvia asks slyly, her head tilted to one side conspiratorially. She has a conspiratorial air to her—always has. No one trusts her. In a family full of large-breasted women she is flat-chested. She giggles incessantly and will never tell what about. She will never marry. No man would ever tolerate her. She has desperately bad teeth.

"It could've been anything. We must all retrace our most recent interactions with her," Father says confidently and we all nod. This is standard procedure. It could have been anything that hurt Mother. She truly is a sensitive woman. There was talk in her early years of her perhaps being an artist although, sadly, no talent was ever uncovered. She excelled at nothing despite being sent all over Europe to all sorts of experts. "She was given the vision but not the gift to express it," is the familiar lament. "We must remember that anything could've caused this," Father reminds us again.

Sylvia, her cool gray eyes suspiciously averted, goes first: "I saw her in the morning. Everything was fine. She was making strudel. [There is a slight rumbling among the group. Mother almost never makes strudel anymore and now Sylvia's whole story has been cast in doubt.] What? She was! She said she wasn't being fair to the younger ones. We all got strudel here and strudel there and Baby and Scotty and Phil never do. And I told her, 'But Mother, all children are different.' But she just sort of looked at me like she does." We all laugh imagining just how

Mother looked at Sylvia and Father butts in. "We are not here to laugh!"

Of course he is right. This is serious business. Mother's been hurt.

Timmy goes next: "I saw her just around lunchtime. She was buttering some rolls for Baby to chew on. She was wearing that housedress that I hate, but I didn't say anything. She looks like such a cow in that thing. Mooo, mooo." Nobody laughs despite Timmy's pleading, snorting looks to join us in his bemusement. We don't laugh because A) Father has just seconds ago reminded us of the gravity of the situation, and B) Timmy has perhaps the least developed sense of humor any of us have ever known—this despite a cinematically comic appearance. The poor lad is saddled with Father's hook nose and Mother's pointy chin—an unfortunate combination the rest of us were happily spared. He's also very nearly idiotic, languishing his days working for the local priest doing idiot chores and running idiot errands (he was once spotted pulling a wheelbarrow full of newspaper down a heavily traveled street) and God knows what else, for which he is paid no money.

It is hopeless. We have all gone over our last encounters with Mother. Hours have gone by. The chips have been reduced to a fine powder of greasy memories on the tips of all our fingers. The grim day has faded into a grimmer night. It could have been anything, anything at all that hurt Mother so. This is the problem with Mother: an offhand remark in one instance might easily fill her with motherly glee, and in the very next—for reasons known only to her and quite possibly *not even* to her—might wound her to the heart.

Thomas, Fred, Lila, Billy, and Steve are playing a joyless game of hearts, perhaps their tenth in a row after having abandoned all hope of getting beyond the disputed points of order their group got hung up on. Thomas and Fred have been reading *Robert's Rules* of late, poring through it in fact, debating its every nuance. Baby and Scotty and Phil have fallen into a deep nap on the couch, sucking each other's thumbs as they generally do. It is quite a sight, this thumb-sucking triumvirate of innocence shot through with a jolting dash of incest. Parlors full of highball-clinking adults have often stood enraptured by the sight of it during Mother and Father's cocktail parties—of which there are many—during which the children often charge about in miniature versions of grown-up gowns and sports jackets sipping from discarded drinks, tugging on trousers and hemlines and falling down drunk and gay. It is a scene we have all played as children.

Our strategy is of no use. I see the inevitable worry seep across Father's furrowed brow. A fine line of sweat forms as he pales. It is he, after all, more so than any of us, who will have to attempt to console Mother from this, the most recent hurt she's suffered. No one has seen her for hours, not since long, long before our meeting began. We can all easily imagine her, lying prone and wounded in a languid sprawl on her favorite crimson divan in the West Parlor with an emptying box of floral scented tissues in her gaily dressed lap listening to cello sonatas and wispily gazing out the French doors past the hulking walnut wardrobe left self-consciously ajar sufficiently to display her collection of her great-grandmother's shimmering sequined evening gowns. It is a painfully familiar sight to us all.

From the depths of our despair Jonas pipes up: "We must cheer her up!" He veritably booms, his striking adolescent face, his enviable bone structure a tragedy in acne. You can not look at poor Jonas without wincing at his decimated skin. No one says anything though. Father discreetly packs him off to see Dr. Raingold, heralded far and wide as the best dermatologist in the world. Still, though, the poor Jonas suffers and in deference to his pain we generally ignore the well-meaning boy. With this though he has attracted all our attention. Cheer her up. Certainly nothing new there, and yet, a simplistic beauty is obvious to us all, coming as it does from the savagely ravaged visage of this young man. Just as we begin to flirt with the idea of feeling a sense of relief, Sylvia, the giggling half-wit, throws in her unwanted two cents. "We *always* try to cheer her up. That's not an idea, that's dumb."

Even in her foulness a spark of truth exists, and our brief tango with hope fizzles sadly. But then Jonas, undefeated, a warrior with a message, his resolve strengthened no doubt from his endless, victoryless battle with his complexion, stands dramatically, pounding the marbletopped table we've been huddled around like a hopelessly hung jury on the late show, pounding it like a Messiah, a man with a vision: "No!" He implores, "No! Do not let the voices of gloom sway you. We may have tried to cheer her before, but have we ever put on a show?!?!" He carries the last syllable of the last word like a well-fed tenor, booming it across the Front East Sitting Room, shaking the other group from its muddled complacency and even waking Baby, Scotty, and Phil, who pull their white and bloodless thumbs from each other's dripping red mouths.

A day passed with only brief sightings of Mother being reported. Billy saw her across the West Rear Parlor, feather-dusting the ponderous oils' rococo frames with slumped and burdened shoulders and a frayed babushka tied around her head in the manner of Southern slaves. Lila insists she saw her brooding in the North Pinetum behind the old caretaker's shack, but this sighting is not considered realistic, as Mother's distaste for pine needles being "tracked all over the house" is legendary. And then Baby, Scotty, and Phil came up with a heartbreaking story on Mother visiting them in their sleep with silver trays full of strudel and popovers, fresh and steaming.

Father will direct the show, about that there was never even the slightest doubt. We admire him more and more as time goes on; the grace with which he carries his burden. He has found an old canvas director's chair amid Grandmother Pearl's collection of memorabilia from her much discussed glory days on the London Stage, which we store on the south side of the East Wing's attic. Also, a cheerleader's bullhorn from Uncle Hal's days at Harvard. The handle's been broken off so Father holds it to his mouth like a giant goblet with both hands. On its side it reads "Harvar," the faded white "d" having dropped somewhere in its dark and musty journey. Thomas tried to get Father to wear riding crops and a pair of knee-high boots, but he balked, thinking he was perhaps being made sport of, something that is always a possibility with the smug and poorly postured Thomas.

My job was to organize the talent or, rather, to uncover it and *then* organize it. I spend the day holding auditions. Thomas and Fred had delusions of re-creating the highlights from the second or third of the Lincoln-Douglas debates with the twist being that they will perform it to improvised music, or, perhaps, a tape loop of "found sounds"—they were still uncertain on that front but seemed to be very much enjoying the discussion, especially saying "found sounds."

Baby, Scotty, and Phil have cooked up a vaudeville routine of scatological humor centering mainly on Baby's overflowing diapers and some exploding cigars they say Sylvia has promised them; complete, of course, with Groucho glasses.

Jonas will juggle two raw eggs and a hatchet. Paul will attempt levitation through chanting. Steve, of course, will bore us all with his tired old impersonations of radio personalities from the thirties that he is forever insisting are uncannily accurate, although none of us have any way of knowing if this is true. (During his audition Father asked him why he doesn't do contemporary stars. "Why not do Leno or Letterman, or even Carson?" he asked. Steve said television personalities were impossible to impersonate with the accuracy he insists upon because you can see he's plainly not Leno or Letterman or Carson.)

Sylvia, aside from providing Baby, Scotty, and Phil with exploding cigars, will sing torch songs from her perch, sprawled ridiculously across the top of the Steinway where she wriggles and moans in mock ecstasy to Lila's amateurish accompaniment. Timmy cries because he cannot think of any talent, any way to cheer Mother. I suggest maybe something he does with the priests and he perks up, returning an hour later with what must be a pilfered silver tray saying he will carry the Host to the altar. Father and I smile and the poor idiot skips away, banging his silver tray into the two-hundred-year-old grandfather clock in the foyer that is ticking away this, the second day of Mother's hurt.

Finally Billy arrives, the last to audition. He too has been to Grandmother Pearl's stash and is dressed in outrageously colored tights and a stocking cap topped with several bells. He says he will recite poetry while performing dangerously complicated tumbles, which he says he cannot possibly demonstrate for us beforehand for fear he may cause himself some serious and permanent injury before the show. Father nods in admiration of his dedication.

Father and I meet in the evening in the West Wing's plush North Study. I have built a fire and we sit in opposite settees before it discussing the show, each of us with a clipboard set neatly before us on our delicately crossed legs. Periodically we are interrupted by Jonas who relays to us Mother sightings. Father takes in the report of each sighting with a resolved sigh, seriously pondering its every implication, searching for some indication, however small, of a thaw, a healing of this mysterious wound. Like all of us he harbors in the recesses of his mind the vain hope that these hurts of hers will just disappear as mysteriously as they appear. The reports are not good, however. Each is vague, wistful. Mother putting in new shelf-lining in the kitchen cabinets. Mother sighing heavily behind drawn parlor doors. Mother feeding the cats. The first and last of these are especially gloomy in that they tell us Mother has discharged the staff and taken to performing household chores on her own—indications of a deep wound.

Our meeting stretches well into the night as we haggle and debate every nuance of the show. Everything must be perfect or we may fail at our task: easing Mother's hurt. The sun's appearance surprises us as the third day of our trial dawns and we make at last our final notes on what will be that afternoon's performance, to be held in the Second Floor's West Drawing Room. We will start with Thomas and Fred's act and work our way downward in age, ending with Baby, Scotty, and Phil's vaudeville number, agreeably the most promising act in the family. Father and I will not perform. He, of course, because he is needed to direct. We discussed the possibility of my performing in the show since now that the talent had been organized I was no longer needed in *that* capacity. I persuaded him, however, that Mother has always disliked my seriousness and the dullness of my features. He made a polite show of protesting this, what we both know to be an absolutely accurate characterization of Mother's feelings toward me, but then he gave in, having done his part. I know I am unappreciated in the family, that my intelligence is resented, my degrees coveted, and my aloofness misinterpreted.

As we stir with the creeping morning sun, Baby, Scotty, and Phil walk in with sleep in their eyes, a trio of toddlers in velour coveralls decorated with ducks and bunnies. Father stokes the dying fire and I stretch, walking to the window, through which I spot Mother off in the distance, like a phantom in the dawn's mist, strolling through the Cherry Orchard, bundled up against the chill, a basket in her arms as she pulls cherries from the trees. It is the first I have seen of her in two and a half days and I feel a frog in my throat at the sighting: gathering fruit at dawn is not good. "We have a full day of rehearsals ahead of us," Father intones as I motion for him and the young ones to come over and in an anxious silence we stare at Mother, oblivious to us all, filling her basket with cherries. Her head tilts to one side, heavy with burden.

Gladys Knows

ONE

Gladys curses her mother under her breath as she pushes a lawn mower across the grass. Eddie, her brother, always makes such straight lines, and yet to do so seems impossible.

The heat is unbearable and Gladys has a hangover.

She needs a cigarette—badly. At the end of every line she stops, sweating, and surveys the strip she's just mowed, invariably finding that she has wavered. Every time. Looking back over the half yard she's done it looks like it was cut by a drunk, a madman, a retard.

Gladys laughs to herself. The grass will need to be emptied soon, before another line is done. Her bra strap is giving her a rash.

In the backyard the Capp twins are digging in the pile of topsoil left by the nursery the weekend before. Gladys sighs, thinking that it'll have to be loaded into the wheelbarrow and spread around the yard into all the various beds her mother dug last weekend with one of the men from the Raw Deal, the bar her father had owned. His name was Jaime and he smoked cigars and worked with no shirt on. He was one of the many men that had been coming over lately.

Like most of them, lately, he was *not* one of the men from the funeral. This is Gladys' main frame of reference with the men that come over for her mother: ones she remembers from the funeral, and ones she doesn't.

Gladys dumps the grass clippings and heads over to see what the Capp twins are doing in the dirt. They are secretive little boys about ten years old who live two houses down. They never dress alike and hate to be thought of as special because of their twinness.

She asks them what they are doing, bent over and smiling her biggest smile. The boys twist their heads up to look at her, squinting into the sun.

"Mind your own business, Barf-bag!" one of them says and they snicker and go back to their digging.

Back in the front yard Gladys is again appalled at her inability to cut even one straight line. The mailman drives by and honks at her as she stands with her hands on her hips regarding her massacre. Billy Walker from up the street walks by—a mess of greasy hair, torn jeans, and nose rings—sucking on a Popsicle and stops to stare at her staring at the grass.

"It's a matter of where you look," he says, coming across the lawn. "If you look directly in front of you as you go, you'll never cut in a straight line. You've got to look to the end of the yard and navigate yourself there."

Gladys tells Billy to fuck off and he shakes his head as if to laugh, the Popsicle stifling any noise. Gladys despises Billy Walker, even though they once had ended up practically fucking out in the woods after a bottle of gin.

"I'm just trying to pass on the wisdom of the suburban sages. Grass cutting is an art, my little Gladys." He grins, knowingly. He begins again, "Like fellatio, it only *seems* easy. Doing it right requires skill."

Gladys says nothing.

The fellatio remark sets her heart pounding. Billy must know that she and Maddox—one of Billy's good friends and Gladys' boyfriend—had a fight last night because Maddox wanted to come in her mouth. She wouldn't let him, though, because she knew he'd screwed Emma after the bonfire the week before. It ended up being a big scene; bigger than it needed to be anyway, and Maddox had almost hit her. He must've told Billy all about it.

Gladys imagines with disgust the conversation *that* must've been.

She glares at Billy, who takes the Popsicle out of his mouth and then shoves it back in . . . takes it out . . . shoves it back in . . . out . . . in. A disgusting leer creeps across his pimply face and then he turns to leave, rolling his head back and cackling.

Gladys reattaches the bag to the side of the lawn mower and pulls the starter. It takes her a couple of strenuous tugs but finally it starts and she turns back to face the yard. She takes a deep breath and then remembers she'd meant to smoke a cigarette after dumping the clippings, but that "Barf-bag" remark from the Capp twins made her forget.

TWO

At dinner Gladys sits in silence while her brother asks their mother if he can bring his new girlfriend over to watch a movie on the VCR.

Mrs. Laker sniffs her peas and says it is a strange time of the year for canned peas. Eddie asks again about his girlfriend, would it be all right if she came over and they watched a movie. "All right?" she says, dramatically arching her eyebrows, pursing her great, painted lips. "All right!? What, so I suppose you can fuck her on the couch. I know what you kids do. Little swine."

Gladys watches Eddie's face recoil from the encounter. She wonders what he expects. It is best not to even mention girlfriends or boyfriends to their mother. The thing to do is to just bring them over and let her make her scene and then have it done with. Once she's done with that you can rely on her to disappear into her room for a good long cry.

Although, lately, she's been calling the Raw Deal; "For company," as she says, "a widow needs that now and then." This is her new thing. Any time of the day or night these men come banging into the house, usually drunk, and they just go right up to her room. Sometimes they stop on their way out and smile at Gladys. Some of them she knows, most she doesn't.

"Well, so I guess it'll be okay then?" Eddie says.

Gladys wonders why he persists.

"Okay? Okay? Since when does anything have to be okay with me around here? Since when has anybody in this house given a good goddamn what I have to say about anything? Bring her over. Screw on the kitchen table for all I care."

Gladys gets dessert from the freezer after dinner. It's some ice cream and cookies her mother mixed together in a fit of inspiration that afternoon after Gladys finished the yard. She'd found her mother in the kitchen in a baggy pair of gym shorts and a white V-necked T-shirt with no bra, sitting at the table in front of a two-gallon jug of vanilla ice cream and two open packs of Oreos. She was mixing them together in a small Rubbermaid bucket. "What would be better?" she said, her eyes thrilled, her hands a sticky mess. "Try and think of one thing better than ice cream and Oreos together," she said. "Just one." Then she went back to mixing it all together with wild abandon.

Gladys was picking up some Oreo wrappings when a man came out of the living room in his underwear. He was holding a basketball tightly to his chest. "Shit," he said. He bounced the basketball once. Gladys glared at him and her mother sucked on her fingers, turning from one to the other. The man bounced the basketball one more time and turned and left.

Eddie whistles as he does the dishes and Gladys dries. She wants to ask him how he always gets the lines so straight when he cuts the grass. Upstairs their mother is singing "High Hopes" at the top of her lungs while rearranging furniture. After dinner she said that it was time to shake up her life with a little redecorating.

"Do you suppose someday she'll just drop dead?" Eddie asks as he rinses the soap out of an ice-cream dish.

Gladys doesn't understand. Everyone drops dead.

"I mean, do you think she'll just run out of energy some day and just stop, like a toy that runs out of batteries or something like that?"

Gladys says she supposes so.

"I picture it sometimes. She'll be going on a rampage, or moving some furniture, or, I don't know, something, one of her *things*, and then she'll just stop, stand straight up, smile once . . . and then just fall down dead. Just like that. It'll all be over."

Gladys is about to tell her brother that he is dreaming, that in the real world people don't just disappear, they linger, they annoy, they take their time exiting. And it's almost never on cue. But then her mother appears, leaping down the steps. She comes bounding into the kitchen, singing, "everyone knows an ant . . . can't . . . move a rubber tree plant . . . but he's got high hopes, he's got high hopes."

She starts dancing around the kitchen table, one hand on her hip, one arched over her head, spinning herself like a music box ballerina. "He's got high apple pie in the sky hopes." Finally she sits down—collapses, really—at the table and sighs a tremendous sigh that leaves her limp and crumpled.

She breathes heavily a few times, pushing the hair from her face. Finally she speaks. "I hate this fucking world," she says, and starts crying, "I hate it more than either of you could ever imagine." Eddie slowly turns the water off—"More then you could imagine in your wildest dreams"—leaving the house in absolute silence.

He and Gladys slowly walk toward their mother, slumped in the chair. As they inch their way across the soiled linoleum, looking back and forth at each other, just as they approach her, she bites her lower lip, lifts her head and says, "Is there any more ice cream?"

THREE

Maddox picks Gladys up in his father's Cadillac. He is all dressed up and has a flower in his lapel and a corsage in a box.

Gladys is surprised, shows it.

"We're going ballroom dancing," he says, pulling out of the driveway.

Ballroom dancing?

"That's right, m'lady, ballroom dancing."

Gladys doesn't know how to ballroom dance.

"There's nothing to it. Besides, the man leads."

Gladys is wearing jeans.

"Fear not."

They get onto the highway and Maddox pulls out a tape and pops it into the stereo. His father's Cadillac has a great stereo system with speakers all over the place and a graphic equalizer built into the dash. (His father is a lawyer and the local judge.) The tape is opera, which at first makes Gladys laugh, but then she sits and listens to it, a soprano with piano accompaniment, and she feels herself relax.

It starts to rain and the drops have a hypnotic effect as she stretches out in the vast American expanse of front seat. She hugs herself into the velour upholstered seat and marvels at the feeling of flight the car offers.

Maddox lights a joint and hands it to her. She inhales deeply and feels the warmth of it in her head. He turns the music up and the car seems to speed up with it. She looks out the window and sees that they are weaving through traffic like magic, like a video game. Lights fly by to the left and to the right, cars part in anticipation of them. It looks as effortless as a walk in the park, and yet they are in two tons of steel and glass.

This feeling of wellness stays with Gladys through most of the joint—through three arias, the beauty of which brings tears to her eyes, makes her spine tingle in a way that reminds her of coming. She feels herself gliding through an unreality as pure as light, as soft as a dream. Even the rhythm of her breathing is harmonious and magical.

Air tastes like sugar, her blood pulses through her veins like the clearest of crystal streams. Her hair feels like silk. The world speeds by like a light show. The world has *become* a light show, as harmless and distant as a laser light show at a planetarium.

She looks over at Maddox and feels a tremendous love for him. She wishes she had let him come in her mouth—he gets such a charge out of it. So what if she couldn't figure out why it mattered *where* he came, if it was *in* or *out* or *on* or *behind* or, who cared, really. The things we let distract us, she thinks, the things we let ourselves be derailed by! She'd let him come in her mouth, she thinks, staring enraptured at him, on Main Street at noon if it would make him happy.

She stares at the side of his face, lit by the halogen street lamps, and her heart pounds for him. The world is perfectly tuned, spinning just as it should. Precisely right. Why had they fought? Just go with it, she thinks, just let it be.

FOUR

But, then, slowly at first, the old familiar anxiety creeps up on her. (She knew it would happen. For months now pot had been making her paranoid.) Suddenly, the shrill screaming voice of the singer begins to grate on every nerve in her body, she feels seasick from the motion of the speeding car. She sees her entire life as one long perilous journey leading up to this one incomprehensibly senseless moment, speeding like lunatics toward a "ball" of some sort—whoever heard of a "ball"?

It is absolutely obvious to her: this is how she will die. It all makes the most perfect sense. Every minute of her long and tortured existence has been leading to this one moment. Her entire history reveals itself to her; it spreads back behind her like a thin, winding path barricaded on each side by tall, sheer walls precluding deviation of any sort. Her death is upon her, her fate is sealed, as it always had been. What a fool she'd been not to know it!

Her body tightens into a knot. She can barely breathe. She pulls her limbs into herself desperately gasping for air.

A scream builds inside her. She feels it starting as a tiny, shrill plea in the bottoms of her feet. And then it builds. And it builds.

By the time it has reached her knees it has become a screech, then it becomes an operatic howl, a desperate guttural cry, a tremendous scathing wail, an inhuman, no a *super*human fantastic scream.

She feels it leaving her mouth against her will, it seems to shatter the interior of the car as it comes, bursting forth. A lifetime's worth of suppressed screams, all of them at once, every scream she never dared scream all her life long, looses itself upon the interior of Maddox's father's speeding Cadillac.

There are immediate results.

Maddox himself picks up the howl, like a contagion. He somehow loses control of the car in the course of his own screaming. Suddenly they are spinning in the rain, the car is spinning uncontrollably across the four-lane highway. They scream and scream. Death is imminent and now both of them know it, so they scream some more. All around them events slow unnaturally.

It was like watching yourself on TV, they will both recount later, *it was like watching a movie.*

They spin to a stop in the grass between the highway's north and south sides. They are unhurt. The car is undamaged. They are out of breath.

"Jesus Fucking Christ," Maddox says, "what the hell was that scream for?"

Gladys can barely open her mouth.

"Jesus Fucking Christ. I think I shit my pants." He is gasping desperately, his eyes so wide it looks to Gladys like they might jump out of his head. "This suit is a rental!"

Gladys notices a foul odor.

FIVE

The Ballroom, a rented party hall really, is decorated with crepe paper and balloons. A spinning mirrored ball hangs from the ceiling. Punch is served by old ladies in taffeta gowns. Maddox and Gladys are the only people under twenty in the entire ballroom. They are the only people under forty, under fifty. It turns out it is an event the police department has put on to raise money for an animal shelter. Maddox's father, as the local judge, got tickets but at the last minute couldn't go because of diarrhea. (Maddox hadn't shit his pants after all.)

Gladys refuses to dance most of the night. She stands in a corner and watches Maddox go from one person to the next, shaking hands, patting shoulders, flirting with old ladies. He will be a politician someday, she thinks. Good family connections, good looks, broad shoulders.

He says he is going to study political science, then law. "I'm a good catch," he told her one night in the back of his car. Gladys was staring off into space, winding and unwinding her bra strap around her middle finger.

Gladys wasn't aware of having cast a line.

SIX

A woman named Chartreuse eventually takes it upon herself to talk to Gladys. It is late and the crowd has thinned out. The band looks bored.

Gladys notices the saxophonist checking his watch. A woman in the corner opposite Gladys, with a crowd of leering men encircling her, is drunkenly trying to recount the Ten Commandments. "Thou shalt not covet . . ." she keeps saying and then giggling.

Chartreuse comes over and shakes Gladys' hand through a white glove. "How do you do?" she asks.

Gladys nods unconvincingly. They introduce themselves and then Chartreuse tells her that she knew her father many years before. "He used to date my Maggie," she says. "This was before he met your mother, of course. He was on the football team. Did you know that?"

Gladys knows.

"Of course you would. He was a fine young man. Very polite, well dressed. Like men were back then. He and my Maggie used to go to the drive-in, to the raceway, picnics. That sort of thing. A very innocent time. Seems almost comical now." Chartreuse looks thoughtfully skyward and continues, "I saw a boy yesterday walking down the street with a red Mohawk and rings pierced through his cheeks."

Gladys smiles. That is Jimmy; an actual suburban heroin user.

Chartreuse shrieks. "My God! Heroin? Really?"

Gladys nods, pleased to have shocked this annoying woman.

"He *injects* heroin? With *needles*?"

Gladys laughs.

"Here in Province? Well, you see what I mean. It was a different world not so many years ago. Your father was a good man."

Gladys thinks about her father, the man that took Chartreuse's Maggie to the drive-in and on picnics. She sees them living in slow motion and soft focus, in a world lit like a douche commercial.

"How long's it been now?" Chartreuse asks, fidgeting as people do, Gladys has learned, when asking about the dead.

"Three years," Gladys says, imagining the spinning pages of a calendar flying off into empty black space.

"To lose someone in a murder is an awful thing. I can't begin to understand what your family must've gone through. And to think it was for, what—what did they get?"

"Forty-six dollars," Gladys recites. People usually act as if it would somehow make sense (or be at least in accordance with their view of the world) if her father's killers had at least stolen some serious money before shooting him squarely in the head, twice. As if a higher figure would allow them a better night's sleep as they fooled themselves into believing that the world makes anything even closely resembling sense.

"Forty-six dollars. Hmmh."

Gladys spots Maddox waving to her from a circle of policemen. When he catches her eye he motions for her to come over. Relieved, she tells Chartreuse her boyfriend beckons.

She looks over toward Maddox and says, very impressed, "Maddox Haines, very good. A girl could do worse."

Gladys shows surprise.

Chartreuse stands up and dusts off her gown. "I always make it a point to tell the young that everything changes. They always seem so sure it won't. That they already know everything. But things change, my dear. Soon much of what you think and feel will be just a memory, a hazy memory. You'll have trouble remembering what it was that you feel so passionately now. About everything."

Gladys has nothing to say.

Chartreuse goes on, patting Gladys' shoulder and smiling broadly. "Many people are crushed by life, a woman my age has seen a lot of people utterly deflated by it," she says. "We shouldn't judge them, though it seems easy. I knew your mother too. She was actually friends with my Maggie at one time. This is a small town."

Gladys imagines its smallness, pretends she is looking at it from above, all the aluminum houses sitting on square plots of green, her yard with its crooked lines.

"To my mind," Chartreuse continues, "that we can even go on, at times, is a miracle. Truly. Up there with walking on water and all that rubbish. That we even find the strength to just go on."

SEVEN

On the way home Maddox teasingly complains that the wife of a politician is supposed to be sociable. "Mix!" he tells her, "Even if you think everybody's an asshole, it's still better to talk to an asshole than to just sit by yourself."

In her defense Gladys says she'd had a lovely talk with Chartreuse.

"She's a nut."

They listen to opera again but don't smoke any pot. When they pass where they'd spun out Gladys feels a chill in her chest. She puts her hand on Maddox's thigh, asks to lie down, she just wants to lie down.

"Whatever," he says.

Gladys moves the armrest and lays her head across the seat onto his thigh. She watches the sky stream past through the windshield and thinks again of flight. She tries to make herself feel the sensation like before, the feeling of everything going smoothly, of the universe being in order. Her head spins, however, and she has to close her eyes.

She turns on her side and strokes Maddox's calf. At home her mother will have some man over. Eddie'll be with his new girlfriend watching one of his super-violent movies. Maybe that is the universe being in order, she thinks. Maybe the universe has no choice but to be in order. Maybe we have a faulty conception of what order is; if we just looked differently and expected something else, not necessarily something less, we'd be okay. She shifts herself a little bit, trying to imagine this new way of looking at things, trying to imagine a Gladys who knows, and yet isn't affected. Maddox begins stroking her hair and fidgeting slightly on the seat. He delicately traces a finger along the line of her jaw and beside her other cheek Gladys feels Maddox getting erect.

The Flood

When I got home from the gym there was a message for the other Jonathan Patrick from a guy named Willie who said he'd had a prophetic dream and absolutely had to talk to me. After that, there was a message from Mona saying that life was a meaningless three-act farce with bad lighting and artistic pretensions. Then there was a lot of laughter and the sound of breaking glass.

I hadn't felt like showering at the gym so I got the water running and put on a tape that Gilroy, my racquetball partner, had made for me. It was a motivational tape he said was absolutely spectacular in a way he couldn't believe. I brought the tape deck into the bathroom and listened to a man with a slight and effeminate lisp named Henry Rodgers Carmel tell me that the world we "create for ourselves" is an almost exact duplication of the world that exists inside ourselves. This, he said, was the key. "Think of the immensity of the universe. Think of the immensity of the subatomic world. What better proof can there be that what exists inside, exists also outside. In all things," Carmel said, "there is harmony."

After the shower I scrounged around the refrigerator and found some leftover pasta Mona had brought over last week. She'd shown up unannounced with a bottle of gin, half empty, and a friend named Clarissa who eyed my computer and stereo all evening (at one point even asking me how much I thought they were worth). I knew I had to call Mona but was dreading it. Fortunately the phone rang and it was Gilroy calling to ask me what I thought of Henry Rodgers Carmel. "The thing I love about him," Gilroy said, "is that he has a sense of humor about what he's saying. He knows how silly it all sounds, but he's still a believer. In my book that's character: Believing in something that's so corny you could puke."

Watching the pasta spin in the microwave I told him I hadn't really had time to listen to all that much of it, but that I would let him know.

"He'll change your life, Jonathan," he said. "You won't look at anything the same."

"That'll be refreshing."

After dinner I called the number Willie left to tell him he had the wrong Jonathan Patrick. His line rang about nine times before I got an answer. I told him the story, that there were two Jonathan Patricks in town. "The one you want," I said, "is the priest on Dillard. I'm the architect on Mallard." I heard nothing but breathing. "I can give you the number if you'd like."

"There will be a flood!" he boomed. "A terrible flood will sweep it all away."

I tried to interrupt, to tell him again that I was the wrong Patrick, but he wouldn't let me.

"It has been revealed," he said. Then, quieter, "It has been . . . revealed." And he hung up.

I called Mona just after "Jeopardy," her favorite show. Everybody knew not to call Mona between seven-thirty and eight. I listened for the clinking of glasses or the sound of anyone else's voice. I knew from her message that she was still drinking. Last week with Clarissa had been her fourth or fifth slip since getting out of rehab two years ago. She seemed to be locked into a vicious game of self-torture. She'd go a few months clean and sober and then, for some reason no one but she could see (if even she could), she'd quit going to her meetings, stop returning phone calls, and then a few days later show up somewhere smashed out of her mind, usually with a woman.

The first time it was with a woman she introduced as Carol at my door. I let them in and Mona asked me if I would hate her if she was a lesbian and then she threw up on my couch. Carol apologized and we sat and had a nice talk while Mona gagged and moaned in the bathroom. Carol was a graduate student in mathematics. She said Mona was sober when they'd met earlier in the evening, but as the night wore on she could see that there was some kind of problem by the way she was gulping her drinks. "I confronted her about it," she said, "and she told me you were the only person who understood her and she made me bring her here." There was a long silence and then Carol said, "She's an old girlfriend of yours?"

I nodded. "We go back a long way."

"Coming out can be very traumatic." As she got up to leave she explained that she wasn't interested in getting involved with someone not completely out. "But if she ever stops needing to be forgiven," she said at the door, "tell her to give me a call."

"When does anyone ever stop needing to be forgiven?"

She stopped for a second, appearing to consider my question seriously, and then said, "Save cute and witty for straight women. You know what I meant."

"Jesus Christ," Mona said, "did you see the final 'Jeopardy' question? My god, it was about Shakespeare—who else? Let's see. It was like, oh, shit, I forgot it already, something about *Timon of Athens*—as if *anyone* knows *anything* about that play. No one got it. I hate Shakespeare," she said, her voice trailing off. "Did you ever stop to wonder what sort of society would have *verse plays* as its most popular form of entertainment? Jesus."

"One very different from this," I said.

"No shit."

Then we talked for a little bit in the random, free-form way I've grown accustomed to with Mona. First she told me about her hedges. "I'm at war with my hedges," she said. "They've got a mind of their own. They scratch me and tear at my clothes, but I'm afraid to cut them back; it's like I think they'll retaliate. I sort of circled them with this big pair of hedge clippers—like the kind you'd see in a slasher movie—for about an hour this afternoon, but I couldn't do it. I got all dressed up like Laura Petrie doing housework, with a babushka and everything." She stopped, waiting for me to respond. "Maybe I'll just move. Jesus, I'm terrified of my hedges!"

In college, when we met, Mona was a sort of campus celebrity. She was beautiful, the daughter of a famous architect, wild, brilliant, and, once, Robert Rauschenberg stayed overnight at her house. I was in my last year of undergraduate studies and was applying to several graduate architecture programs when we met. I'd seen her around campus for three years and knew her by reputation, of course, but didn't become friends with her until we had a class together that year. It was a literature class I'd neglected to take as one of my electives: Female Writers of the Twentieth Century. Mona hated everyone we read, refused to acknowledge any of them as worthy. She seemed to love antagonizing the professor, a very young woman who didn't know what to make of Mona. "Christ," she'd say, "tell me what *is* good about Virginia Woolf. *To the Lighthouse* is so dense and incomprehensible it's like swimming in mercury. I guess she's following Joyce; blundering along behind the male lead, like a good little minor modernist. Absolute garbage."

I admired her tenacity. Over the years, it had become less appealing.

After telling me about her hedges she said, "Oh, and Uncle Fuck says he's going to court to keep me away from the principal until I can—what did he say?—demonstrate emotional soundness, or something like that." Uncle Fuck was what she called the trustee of her trust fund. Her parents evidently still had some control over the principal and were not very happy about the way she'd been frittering away the money since dropping out of school.

"Be outraged, Jonathan," she said, "you're not outraged enough."

"How could he?" I said, as blasé as I could, the irony tickling her.

"God I hate my life," she said with a laugh and then told me her mother was an emotional terrorist and that her brothers were gathering a posse to take control of her pussy. "They're gathering up a pussy posse and they're going to drive across the international date line and plant a flag in my crotch, claiming it for *mankind*. They've decided its best only men go sniffing down there."

That semester in college we became good friends and even slept together for a while, but dropped that at Mona's insistence. She said sex was bourgeois and demeaning. "All that licking and sucking! Good lord!" I didn't mind because I was just enthralled to be so close to someone who at the time struck me as being absolutely free. Also, I suppose, I was thrilled to be so close to the daughter of such a famous architect. "You want to meet Daddy?" she would taunt. "He's a drunk," she'd say. "And sleeps around. With boys, I think."

In June, as I was graduating, Mona dropped out and went to Alaska for a year. I got three letters from her while she was gone. She was working at "an assembly line of death. Salmon get carried by on this conveyor belt and my job is to slice open their bellies and squeeze out their guts. Twelve hours a day, six days a week. We all get drunk every night and live in tents and stink like you can't believe."

I lost track of Mona for a while and then she showed up in

Denver and rented a little house in the suburbs. We would see each other sporadically, sometimes being in near constant contact for months at a time, then she would sort of disappear for a while. We had both done a lot of drinking at school, and I assumed that she, like most people, had let it trail off afterward. But then about two years ago she ended up in an emergency room. She'd been drinking downtown and passed out in an alley in a driving October rainstorm. Her parents flew out and her father told her that the money would absolutely be taken away unless she went to a rehab. She got out looking better than I'd seen her look in years; since college maybe. She went to AA meetings, had a sponsor, read me passages of the Big Book over the phone ("Some of us exclaimed, 'What an order! I can't go through with it!'"), laughing about how bad the writing was ("It's *worse* than a fifth-grade textbook."), but believing, I thought, the message.

Then the slips started. She had about six months and she picked up. With a vengeance. She drank for about a week and called me every night, screaming at me about all the ways I'd failed her, how I'd used her to get her father to write me a letter of recommendation to Yale (he did, and I got in), how cheaply my success had come since graduating (I was an associate partner in a nice-sized Denver firm), and, worst of all, how I'd abandoned what she called "the vision."

"You used to be someone, you know," she'd say, "you used to actually have 'the vision.' Most people give it up, I know, but watching you, *you*, bite the apple, well . . ."

I didn't start hanging up on her until the fourth or fifth day. Then I didn't hear from her until about a month later when she called me sober to do an eighth step; asking for my forgiveness.

"I'm crazy," she said, genuinely humble, her voice cracking. "I don't know what to say. You're my only friend."

"It's okay, Mona."

I could hear her sniffling, sobbing. "Did I say something to you, uhm, about 'the vision'?"

"Yes," I said. "Seems I've lost it."

"Oh, Christ."

After her second or third slip, I told her it seemed to me that it was too bad she'd ever gotten sober at all; that the rehab had turned her drinking from a problem into a nightmare. "Stop torturing yourself," I told her. "If you have to drink, for God's sake, drink, but do you have to disembowel yourself in the process?"

"There are worlds, my love," she'd said that time, darkly for effect, "whole *worlds* of agony you couldn't begin to guess at."

Tonight, though, I didn't particularly feel like getting into it with her so I told her about Henry Rodgers Carmel, how he believes we create our own reality.

"Oh, gag!" she said. "Puke, puke and double puke. That's so American. Only an American could believe something that shallow." There was a pause, I heard her drinking something. "Why do you suppose the Rwandans and the Bangladeshis have created such hell for themselves?" Another pause, followed by a deep inhaling of cigarette. "Boy, you know, if you think about it, this tape could end the need for international aid as we know it. All we have to do is tell the unwashed masses to change their attitudes. Imagine how thrilled they'll be. Christ. Americans are the most idiotic, self-absorbed creatures ever to pollute this earth."

That night I listened to the rest of Henry Rodgers Carmel's tape. He spoke of all sorts of "truths" about harmony and synchronicity and how the outer world is a projection of individual inner reality. He said that we take tiny images and ideas we have about ourselves and blow them up until they become our reality. He had all sorts of evidence backing this claim up, some of it anecdotal, some of it very technical "proof" he claimed from the field of quantum physics. He spoke very hypnotically, with a force and conviction I admired, stopping every now and then to remind his live audience, which was very receptive to these ideas, that everything, every single thing, was entirely—"That's right, entirely"—up to them. "You are the creator," he said, "just as surely as you are the created."

I fell asleep sometime around midnight.

The next day it started raining. I woke to a frightening thunderclap a split second before the alarm rang. I had a big meeting on my mind and didn't think anything of Willie's prophecy. I had lunch with Gilroy after the meeting, which was with a hostile zoning commissioner about a strip mall we were designing for a new developer in town. We ran across the rapidly flooding street to a little Chinese place. Gilroy had a crush on one of the waitresses, the only non-Asian in the place, and, as always, he flirted with her as we ordered.

He couldn't wait to talk about Henry Rodgers Carmel. "So?" he said, sipping the ice water and dropping the napkin into his lap, "what did you think?"

I told him that it was very interesting, but that although I was no expert in particle or quantum physics, some of the science seemed pretty dubious.

"Science schmience," he said. "What about the rest of it; about how we create reality? That seems right on target to me."

I said it was probably partially true and was the kind of thing expressed in truisms like "You are what you pretend to be, so be careful what you pretend to be." I also said that his account didn't really explain suffering. I told him about what Mona had said about Rwanda and Bangladesh. "I mean, pick a global tragedy. The Holocaust. Cambodia. East Timor. Whatever." Gilroy nodded, smiling oddly. "I mean, it's one thing to say middle-class Americans choose to be successful and happy or miserable failures, but the Jews going to the gas chambers? I mean, come on. Most of them," I said as our soup arrived, "probably had other expectations."

"It's interesting that you bring that up," he said. "That's what he covers in a different tape. He says those sorts of global catastrophes are abstractions and, as far as individual souls are concerned, are really irrelevant." Gilroy held up his hand to stop my protest. "Just wait. Maybe hundreds of thousands of Hutus were killed by the Tutsis, or whichever was doing the chopping, but each death, each life, *by itself*—that's what matters." Gilroy was enjoying himself immensely, leaning on the table with his elbows.

"This is what he says. He's talking to a live audience as usual, and when he gets to this part, about the Holocaust and those things, everything gets real quiet and he says basically what I just said: that looked at in the whole it's difficult to understand, but that that's not the way to look at it. He says, and it's deathly quiet, 'It's one life at a time, one death at a time.' He says that each person walking into the gas chamber had his own story and so did each guard. The collective cruelty is for historians and politicians to struggle with."

"That's not an answer," I said.

Gilroy shrugged and spooned a wonton into his mouth. "What do you want from me?" he said with his mouth half open. "You want me to tell you why the Jews were gassed? Here? Today? Over lunch?"

"It would be nice."

He looked at me kind of cockeyed. "Listen," he said, "you ever read the Book of Job? You want to talk about suffering, there's the guy to talk about. I had a shrink once who told me to read it when I was going crazy about this woman that dumped me in architecture school. Beautiful girl, rich as hell. Anyway, my shrink says, 'Go read Job.' And I did because I was about as miserable as a person gets and I've always sort of secretly wanted to have a religious experience—like the fundamentalists talk about. Can you imagine that? To *know* God is present in your body? Yikes!" He imitated shivers running through his body. "So anyway, I read it and there are no answers there. It's pure narrative. Job suffers, he complains, God's resolve remains, Job acquiesces. No answers. A straight chronology. It's absurd. I stopped seeing that shrink."

"You've lost me, Gilroy."

"The point is, the Bible doesn't have an answer for suffering except 'Get used to it and stop complaining.' So what do you expect from me? I can't help it that suffering for me doesn't mean life and death questions. I just want to learn to relax and be happy. Is that so bad? I have no idea why the Jews were gassed, or why the Bangladeshis die by the thousands in typhoons, okay?" The waitress walked by with dinners for the next table and Gilroy stopped and watched her every move, slowly wiping his napkin across his chin. He turned to me and rolled his eyes and smiled. "Man," he said. "Would you just *look* at that ass." He paused, looked again, and turned back to me. "Just try and empty your mind, my friend, and *look* at that woman's ass!"

It continued pouring for the next two days. On the third day, the networks sent video crews. Fire trucks began regularly plowing through the flooding streets. Grocery stores were filled with frightened, wet people stocking up on supplies. There was an emergency declared and officials came on TV, actually using the emergency broadcast system, and said things would be taken care of, steps were being taken, plans were being drafted, and funds were being set aside to assist those who had lost everything. Such people were interviewed in tents overflowing with children and cots. Their faces were blank as they recounted litanies of loss.

The third day of the flood was a Saturday, and I called Father Patrick. I'd been thinking about him and Willie's prophecy since the rain started getting serious. It took me a couple of tries to get him. He was out at a rec center helping set it up as an emergency shelter. We'd spoken several times over the years, exchanging messages, and I always enjoyed talking to him.

"Jonathan," he said. "How nice to hear from you. What's up?"

"It's about a call," I said, feeling vaguely foolish. "I got this call the other day."

"Another lost soul with a wrong number?"

"Not exactly." I cleared my throat. "It was from a guy named Willie. He left a message saying he had to talk to me, meaning you, and that it was urgent. So I called him back to give him your number."

"That was nice of you."

"Huh? Yeah, well, yeah. So I called him up and he sounded sort of, well, unbalanced."

"We get a lot of them."

"And he said he'd had a vision that there was going to be a terrible flood. He said it had been revealed." There was silence on the other end. "Father?"

"Oh, I'm sorry, someone was distracting me over here. You say he said there would be a flood? Hm." He laughed and I heard a loud crash in the background. "I guess he was right."

"Well, yeah," I said. "He was more than right. He was *right*. He saw the future. Don't you find that odd?"

Father Patrick shouted something at someone and then returned to the phone. "Jonathan, I'm sorry, but I've got to get back to these people here. I think they emptied an insane asylum for the helpers. Over *there*!" he shouted to someone. "Call me later. I'll be back at the rectory this evening. And don't worry. There are more prophets roaming this earth than anyone will ever record. Happens every day. You've probably seen the future several times yourself, eh? You just don't go calling priests about it."

On the fourth night of the flood Mona showed up soaking wet at my door. She was dressed in yellow rain gear from head to toe and was carrying a cat. "It's the end of the world," she said pushing past me. "This is Trigger. I found her on the roof this morning. We braved Armageddon to commiserate."

The storm seemed to be getting worse. It was thundering almost continuously. Long streaming bolts of lightning broke the darkness with bursts of blue and red and orange, and, most frighteningly, white. The electricity had been going off and on all day and people were being advised to prepare for a massive evacuation, should it become necessary.

"There's one good thing about this storm," Mona said, "my brothers and their pussy posse can't get here."

My apartment was lit entirely by candles. Mona pulled a bottle of wine from her coat. I sighed and shook my head. "Please, Mona," I said, "not tonight."

"The world is ending," she said. "There's a little-known clause in the Big Book about alcoholics being allowed to drink during the end. And this is the end. Why stay sober?" She was speaking in a voice of forced carelessness, which she had when drinking, as she tore at the foil around the top of her wine, struggling very intensely with it.

"I wish you would just stay sober," I said. "Why can't you just stay sober?" I asked, for probably the hundredth time.

She stopped peeling for a second and looked up, as though this was a profoundly intriguing question, and I knew she would savage my intention with sarcasm. "Hm," she said. "Why can't I just stay sober? Very interesting question. Let's think about that for a second."

"Oh, just forget it," I said and got up to look out the window.

My apartment was on the fourteenth floor and I could see much of the town from my balcony. It was still pouring rain and I could see flashing lights and hear sirens all over the place. Down in the street I saw a group of emergency officials huddled under the awning of the small condominium complex across the street. They were all in yellow rubberized suits and held walkie-talkies. They looked to be shouting at each other, arguing about something. I noticed Mona was still talking as Rickie, the super of my building, ran across the street to join the huddle. My street was flowing with about a half a foot of water. I thought I saw the body of a dog go floating around the corner.

I took a deep breath and turned back to Mona. I said I wouldn't be surprised if we were evacuated soon. "They aren't going to just let us stay here."

"What business is it of the state," she asked, "to tell us we can't stay here? If I want to stay in my house—or in this case, your house—that's up to me, isn't it? Why is everybody always fucking with you?"

I twisted the blinds shut and tried to imagine all the chaos away, thinking of Henry Rodgers Carmel. "I wish I knew," I said, looking at Mona struggling to open the wine, biting her lower lip in concentration. I sat down behind her on the couch and began patting her head. She leaned back into me and sighed as I pulled her hair into a ponytail. "We're going to at least use glasses, aren't we?"

She beamed and said, "You're going to join me?" I nodded and she cheered and dashed into the kitchen with her arms raised in victory to get two wine glasses. When she came back I smiled and asked her what all this talk was about the pussy posse. She told me that she had called her mother one night, "very drunk," and told her that she was a lesbian. "I think I may have actually described my taste for eating pussy." She smiled at me. "In graphic detail."

"Anyway," she said, "the next day my brother Glen called. I've told you about him. He's a plumber's assistant in Morristown, New Jersey?" I shook my head. "Very odd guy. He essentially stopped talking when he was fifteen. Everyone used to comment on it. He was this fairly normal teenager, and then he just dummied up. Shut down. My parents sent him to several shrinks. It was very odd. He left home after high school and moved to New Jersey. He's got a trust just like mine, but he's never once used it! Can you believe it? I mean it would be one thing if he rejected it out of principle, but this is like rejecting it out of mental illness." Mona's mouth was agape in disgust.

"Anyway, he left home and went to a trade school and got this job as a plumber's assistant, and that's what he's been doing for like nine years now, in near total silence. So anyway, they've all decided to meet at Michael's in Oak Park and then drive out here. I think they wanted to drive to sort of add to the drama, give it a buddy movie kind of feel. They're probably in a hotel in Nebraska right now," she said, "playing poker on a bedspread and drinking whiskey."

She'd had a blast telling the story and afterward reclined back against the couch, downing her wine in big gulps. Trigger, the cat, was drying out and starting to explore the living room, tentatively sniffing at a candle. There was something in the air that made me tense. I had a very bad feeling about the storm and got up to go look out the window. "Watching it won't affect it," Mona called as I pulled open the blinds. "Just do like me: pretend it's not happening." I looked back at her, smiling. "Don't laugh. It's a very effective strategy."

I closed the blinds and returned to the couch. "There," she said. "See how easy that is?" Mona refilled her glass for the third time and I stretched out on the couch. She pulled the tie out of her hair and let it fall around her shoulders. She looked beautiful and absolutely relaxed. "God," she said, cradling herself in her arms and wiggling her toes, "if only you could just feel like this all the time, like you do after half a bottle of wine."

Congressman Spoonbender

The office phone has not rung in more than an hour and the Legislator finds himself distracted by its silence. He feels cut off, and then, for a disquieting instant, he questions the truth of his own existence without confirmation from beyond. He thinks of his undergraduate days, the overwhelming uncertainty that seemed to define that lost and hollow time. The endless inner probing. "Do I exist, don't I exist." The philosophy texts of the time. They'd called it existentialism and they'd forced it down his young impressionable throat. What a thing to do to people who are essentially still reeling in a profound postadolescent funk: To teach them that nothing is certain or knowable, not even your own existence! No wonder there was so much drug abuse and stringy, unkempt hair on campuses. Existentialism, ha! Another instance of some pushy European intellectual infecting the God-given optimism of the American heart.

He makes a note to work these thoughts into a speech. Is education an issue he's interested in? Is the media ordering that soup these days? He can't think why not, but probably they are not. He makes a note to Janice, his media person. He picks up his phone and dials the number of his mistress, back home in Xenia.

"Cahhh-ngressman," she says, deeply, playfully drawing out the syllables as she does, luxuriously embedded, the Legislator imagines, in her leather couch; Lysol, her cat, on her lap, a Shermans burning in her tinfoil ashtray. "How runs the government?"

"Perilously," he says. "Things have changed, you can feel it in the hallway, see it, even, in the eyes of the pages. No reverence. And the conversation in the elevators." The Legislator stops, thinks, "Have you been on the elevators here?"

"Of course, darling, your precious elevators, hmh."

The Legislator tries to remember when his mistress had been to the Capitol, rode the majestically appointed elevators. The brass fixtures, the plush blue carpeting, the soundless ascents and descents. He continues, "Even *they* have changed. No one speaks." He pauses, cocks his head, "Even the lobbyists seem timid."

"Hmh," the Legislator's mistress says, as he senses he is losing her interest. He knows she hates these sorts of discussions. This life he leads in the nation's capital is of no interest to her. "Timid lobbyists, you say? Sounds like a Sri Lankan diplomat." The Legislator's mistress scoffs. Inhales. The Legislator tenses. "Like a medieval dance craze . . . A disease of the lower abdominals. A . . ."

The Legislator cuts her off. He has begun to perspire. "We are on the brink, I think." A vast silence. "As a nation."

On the other end of the line, a television clicks on, something carbonated is twisted open. "You'd never know it in Xenia." She huffs, scoffs, moves on the couch. "Hold on a second, congressman." The phone falls to the carpeted floor. The Legislator hears shuffling feet, a giggle, a cat's meow. She returns to the phone, out of breath. "Here's a story for you: I found a fifty-dollar bill today in a pair of jeans. Just as I was about to wash them. I bought two pounds of organic wild rice, an old Prince CD—from that bizarre paisley stage he went through—and three joints from a twelve-year-old kid next door. I don't *ever* remember having a fifty-dollar bill. Who carries fifty-dollar bills?"

"I'm writing a speech," the Legislator says, looking again out his window at the sprawling length of democracy that lay beyond. "I feel . . ."

The Legislator's mistress is getting another call, and she says, "Congressman, hang on, it's the other line," and the Legislator is put on hold by his mistress in Xenia.

Did she say "joints"?

The hum of the phone reminds the Legislator of fluorescent lights, of faded linoleum and peeling paint. He sighs for the world in its fallen state, so apparent when on hold.

"Congressman, it was the homeless people, they wanted to know if they could rely on me this spring. It was a very nice young woman, sounded black—is that a racist comment? She did nonetheless. I told her that spring just wouldn't be spring without giving to the homeless."

"I feel a doom, my love, an absolute doom . . ."

The line goes dead. The Legislator hangs up and turns to his desk. The swivel mechanism of his plush leather chair is squeaking and, worse, offering resistance to the whimsy of his spinning. He repositions his legal pad on his desk and sets in motion the rack of suspended ball bearings on his desk that was given to him by the leader of a delegation of businessmen from Kuala Lumpur, a city in a country that the Legislator had always imagined was nothing but jungles and headhunters and unexplained ferry accidents, but which turns out to in fact be an up-and-coming capitalist power. The man's name, the Legislator remembers as he stares at the clicking, swinging ball bearings (dancing a ballet of energy conservation and transference he cannot really claim to understand but likes to think nonetheless that he does), was Herman and he stood about five foot two and had skin a darker black than the skin of the people Americans call "black." He was very nearly purple, the Legislator thinks.

The Legislator flips a lever positioned on the side of his desk and the stereo bursts on. The classical music station is playing a symphony by, the announcer tells him in a quiet, knowledgeable tone that the Legislator finds irritating in an extreme way, Sibelius. Another depressing European infecting the hopeful sanctity of the American spirit. He presses a button for the soft favorites station and finds a pleasing beat, a hopeful melody, words meant to reassure him (if only they could!) that his experience is much like everyone else's here on this sad but really quite lovable little blue planet spinning through an emptiness in space the size and significance of which perhaps one brain in two million is capable of fully comprehending, but that needn't even be thought about, really, what with such things as the blushing sentimentality of young love set to uplifting music just a radio dial away, begging us to let it spin its distracting spell.

The Legislator wonders about the nature of the flaw that separates him from his fellow man, that churns the inside of his brain as it does. What has he done to deserve such exile? He feels at times a separate being lives inside him, poisoning his mind. In earlier years he imagined his anxiety marked him as an artist, an intellectual: for weren't they also plagued by ringing emptiness of eternity? Wasn't the source of artistry breathless despair at the plodding, the endless, the *steamrolling* circularity of history? Isn't that what he'd been taught? Maybe not in so many words, but the message'd been there, of that much the Legislator was sure. The years he'd spent purging himself of such nonsense!

He thinks now of the gnawing in terms of biblical metaphor, a dark force of evil occupying this earth and tormenting the minds of Man with such foolishness, in clear defiance of the will of God, God who is the Creator. He shudders at the clarity of the image, its truthfulness. He moves his decorative pen holder to the right corner of his desk and in its place puts his combination American and state of Ohio flag holder. He loosens his tie and then retightens it. He clears his throat, the noise frightening him, so distant does it seem.

The Legislator sits back in frustration. His body feels heavy to him, unnaturally dense, as if his blood has turned to mercury. He lifts his arms, one after the other. He is definitely heavier than he was yesterday—even, it seems, than he was ten minutes ago. He calls up his mistress.

"Cahhhh-ngressman," she says. He hears running water and the clanking of dishes. He imagines her at the sink, the cordless phone cradled between her freckled shoulder and the side of her delicate head. Her hands he sees in the sink covered with suds and turning slightly red from the heat. "We're not going to discuss doom or gloom again are we?"

"No."

"Or that Sri Lankan diplomat?"

"No."

"The tone of the hallway in that ghastly marble building of yours?"

"No."

"Good, then, my pet, my sweet committeeman. Talk to me."

The Legislator turns to look out his paneled window. He can see far off in the distance the skeleton of a new office tower, men in yellow helmets all over it. He tells his mistress about it, he describes every detail, and as he does so he becomes fascinated by the intricacy he is able to discern—even from such a distance. He notices there is an elevator that is in near constant motion to the side of the building. He tells his mistress that, looking at it, he can almost *feel* himself out there on those beams, among all those machines and pulleys and cables. He tells her it is a fascinating world, where people have such varied experiences. "There are people, thousands of them—tens of thousands, if not hundreds of thousands—for whom climbing around the girders of under-construction skyscrapers is commonplace, a barely worth mentioning experience." When he is done he hears the water shut off at her end. "Done with the dishes?" he asks.

"I was cleaning bones, Congressman, not dishes. The little one is bringing bones in to school tomorrow."

The Legislator is stunned by this revelation. He feels a pain in his ear and opens the leatherbound atlas of the ancient world given to him by a lobbyist for the sugar industry. "I guess I should go now," he says, looking at a misshapen rendering of the New World. "I've got a speech to write."

The line goes dead.

The Legislator is overcome with melancholy. Hearing of his mistress' little one ties a knot in his abdomen and then for some reason he revisits his own childhood, imagining the pools of undoubtedly tepid water he and his young friends used to splash in. He recalls the animals they used to torture and kill, the newts and salamanders whose heads he would crush between his thumb and forefinger, the bones he used to play with, and he finds himself stunned, as if he's uncovered old newsreel footage of graft, or crimes against humanity: the enduring images of the Legislator's childhood continue to haunt him well into the fifth decade of his life, and he shakes his head that such is the case.

He consults the atlas a final moment and closes the book, admiring the solidity of the book itself and his forebears' attempt to draw a picture of the world without the benefit of flight to get the shapes right. He thinks about the task and can't begin to imagine how it was done. How does one draw a coastline while walking it?

The country, he thinks again, is in great peril. He knows this as surely as he has ever known anything. Democracy itself, that bold ideal emblazoned in the soul of each and every American for generations and generations, is on its deathbed. His heart races imagining it go, seeing it off, mourning its death. He has heard from his people who talk to the people, and they tell him that there is a revolt brewing. Janice, his media person, says that often people "desire" dictatorship, that there are in fact many well-researched papers published in respected journals of thought suggesting that what we have come to know as democracy may not be the most efficient means for controlling society. "Face it," Janice says, "a *change* won't mean anyone's going to be setting up any gulags in Rhode Island. There are efficient ways to organize society," she says, coldly, as Janice says things, "and there are inefficient ways. Look at Singapore. You don't see people bellyaching about freedom. They've got jobs, money, safety. This is what real people want. Only intellectuals worry about freedom."

The Legislator takes out his tape recorder and records a few thoughts about the coming era in the hopes that historians will be able to learn something. He watches the plastic reels spin, the tape collecting to the left side as the machine hisses and the feet counter spins ridiculously slow. After ninety seconds he shuts the machine off and begins breathing normally again. History frightens him, like having someone standing at the next urinal. He tells himself that his is important work and looks out his window to remind himself who he is and where he works. He clears his throat as though someone were listening.

Minutes pass. The Legislator checks to see that he is in fact alone—even though he *knows* that he is—and, tightening his eyes into a grimace, tries to move a pen across his desk using only the power of his mind—something he has tried to do probably once a day, at least, since his early teens when he read a book about Uri Geller, the great Israeli psychic, the bender of spoons. He is almost certain he doesn't have any telekinetic powers, but who knows, someday it might turn out that he does. The world is unimaginably complicated and mysterious and not a single person in it can say for sure that they understand it all.

Incredibly, the pen does not move.

His secretary, the Ph.D. candidate, is on vacation in, of all places, the Philippines. His office feels warm to him, unnaturally warm, and there is a foul odor. He wishes he could press the button on his phone marked "Sec" and have her answer him. Maybe she could explain things to him, help him resolve his doubts. He pictures a globe, imagining where he is and where his secretary is. Almost completely opposite sides of the sphere. How is that possible? She is writing a dissertation on "Peoples and Lands as War Booty in the Great Colonial Period: The Story of the Philippines." She is in a library he guesses, on that rocky, jungle-ridden archipelago turning the pages of some thick dusty book. He is in his office thinking about her. He wonders if in thinking about her, picturing her in the striking visual fantasy world in his head, he has an effect, any sort of effect, on her essence or being or soul or energy. He doubts it and would in fact bet against it but the thought entertains him and inflates his sense of importance and this is something the Legislator enjoys.

The sky is dull gray. He picks up the coffeemaker and examines the stains that circle its rim. A large, fist-sized knot grows in his abdomen as he imagines his death, the world going on after him, the cool silence of eternity whispering relentlessly in his ears. Will there be reward for all that we endure? Will anything be explained? The questions torment him, hijacking what little peace he has managed to accrue.

The Legislator picks up the phone and dials his mistress. He is stunned by the beauty of her voice. "I can't get away from you this evening," she says, and then she takes a sip of something.

"What are you drinking?" he asks, running his pudgy fingers through his unwashed hair.

"A sloe gin fizz. My second since dinner. I'm waiting for 'Hard Copy.' I feel like getting drunk and cheering the paparazzi." She takes another sip.

The question he wants to ask her chews at his guts. He finds in her, his mistress in Xenia, such composure, such certainty. He blurts it out: "How do you *know* anything?"

"How do *I* know anything?"

"One. How does *one* know anything?"

The Legislator hears his mistress inhale deeply, holding in her breath. There follows a silence and then the Legislator hears his mistress tell the little one to run upstairs for a second. He thinks he hears her grind out a cigarette—is that possible?—as she waits for the little one to leave; the phone, it sounds like, is held to her chest. She brings it back to her mouth to speak and he can almost smell the gin, see the drops of water dripping down the side of the glass. "Certainty, my sweet, exists independently of its conscious realization. Surely you must understand that? It's the degree to which you are convinced of its existence that matters." Silence. "You're asking the wrong question. What you should be asking is: 'Is there certainty?' To which the answer, obviously, is 'Yes.' You're splashing around in the murky waters of *how* one recognizes it in the mind, which is an indescribable act of will, purely volitional. Certainty *exists* in the mind precisely at the moment it is acknowledged." Purposeful exhalation. "It can't be explained or dissected, just acted upon." She pauses, and sips from her second sloe gin fizz. "It goes like this, my sweet, baffled legislator, my drafter of laws: belief plus action equals certainty, certainty draws a crowd, and in numbers, my dear, *history* is made."

The Legislator is taking notes. There is a knock on his door, a clandestine knock if ever he has heard one. The Legislator cups the phone in his hand and says, "Yes?" A uniformed head pokes in, smiling, and the Legislator holds up his index finger and nods his head to the phone in his hand. The military man signals his understanding and retreats to the reception room, the door closing with a sturdy, congressional thud behind him. The Legislator returns to the phone.

There is a distant, oceanic hum in his ear. He has grown aroused and shifts uncomfortably in his seat. "What are you wearing?"

"Crotchless panties, fire engine red. Sequined bustier." There is a pause. "Old gray sweats I've been farting in all evening." There is another pause. "What was the question?" She laughs, bursts really. The Legislator is puzzled and hears the grinding of metal on flint, the small burst of flame of a disposable lighter and the breath of his mistress in Xenia being drawn through a thick brown Shermans. The line goes dead.

The military man returns and removes his hat. He has a gleam in his eyes. He tells the Legislator that everything he has ever read in a history book, every single event, started out as an idea in the brain of one man.

The Earthling!

Myrna usually showed up around midnight. The first few times she pretended to be working on something. She would sit at one of the computer terminals the shop rented out at ten dollars an hour and she would push the keyboard aside and start frantically writing on soggy graph paper. Every hour or so she would get up and make a couple of copies. People would come and go, mostly students; some would look over at her, most would not. There was clearly something wrong with her; you could see it in the empty panic in her eyes and if you couldn't see her eyes you could guess it from her raggedy clothes. Around three in the morning she'd fold her arms on the counter, rest her head in her arms, and go to sleep.

There was a regular group of street people who came in all during the night. The manager told me that the best way to deal with them was to be what he called "firm but polite." The company, which operated twenty-four-hour copy shops all over the world, even circulated a pamphlet on the subject called "Dealing with the Homeless." It said that there were cities where the copy shop would be the only thing open in the middle of the night, but that that didn't mean it was okay for people to loiter. "Remember," it said, "we are here to offer a service to paying customers, many of whom are in a hurry and need high-quality, professional assistance. Don't let yourself—or your store—be distracted." The pamphlet featured a picture of a clerk standing by a store window, lit with an Open 24-Hours neon sign, a pitch darkness beyond.

I didn't mind the street people. It got pretty dull in there in the middle of the night, so I would let anyone come in, as long as they weren't loud or dangerous looking. There were several regulars that I got to know fairly well over the year I worked there. Some were mentally ill, some were drunks or drug addicts, all seemed pretty harmless. I taught one or two how to use a Macintosh and showed them the fun things you could do with Quark and PageMaker and TypeStyler. I'd take their pictures with the Polaroid we used for passport photos and then scan it and make them stationery with their picture at the top. There was a guy who carried around huge plastic bags of used clothes that he would sell to whoever would take the time to look at them. I made him a big poster on the Zoomer with his face in the center encircled with the words "Clothesman: He Gots What You Wants" in ridiculous Old English script—the font he chose from the hundreds I showed him.

Another guy (who wasn't homeless but seemed pretty destitute) I taught how to create fraudulent paycheck stubs just like the ones he got from his job but with larger numbers so he could get a loan. I helped another couple of middle-aged drunks write letters to the department of commerce to secure funding for an aid program the government ran to assist minority businessmen import products from underdeveloped countries. I helped them make impressive-looking stationery for a fictional importing company.

The guy I helped with the pay stubs got his loan, the importers stopped coming in. Clothesman disappeared for a while and then showed up looking strung out and smelling so bad I had to make him leave. Still, I liked them all, and when I got together with friends, I would tell them stories about these people I'd met on the night shift at the copy shop.

Among them, Myrna was unique. For one thing, she was the only woman and the only white person who slept in there. She was tiny, barely over five feet and had short blonde hair and Nordic features. She carried a colorful backpack crammed full with books, notebooks, cigarettes, and food. Sometimes she would hum to herself, but she was basically no trouble and I felt good to be providing a space for her. I wished there was something else I could do for her, but except for having no home and being mentally ill, she seemed pretty well taken care of. She never asked for money, often came in with a Subway sub and big two-liter bottles of Coke. She clearly had had an education, judging from the worn Kazantzakis and Hesse paperbacks that were sometimes sticking out of her bag, and other than giving her a place to sleep, I couldn't think of any way to help her. In the morning, before Julio (the first-shift guy) came in, I'd vacuum or do something else loud that would "accidentally" wake her and she'd lift her head up. In a minute or two, she'd pack up her stuff and walk wearily out the door.

The first time I ever heard her talk was one night after she'd been coming in fairly regularly for about a month. I was sitting behind the counter and suddenly, and with great glee, she shouted a question across the store. She said, "Tell me: What do you think of the country club mentality of the Palermo Italians?" I was reading the *New York Review of Books*. There were several other people in the store and everyone's attention turned to me.

"Why," I said, smiling brightly, "I think it's deplorable," and I looked around the store, meeting nothing but smiles.

"I know several Palermo Italians here in America. There was a count of French origin who owned a castle I used to stay at."

Her eyes were wide and sad and I sensed, or flattered myself that I sensed, that she understood herself to be speaking nonsense and was shocked yet resigned to these meaningless words falling out of her mouth. I thought I saw a struggle going on in her head to push away a tremendous fog that was mutilating her intentions in ways she couldn't begin to understand or control. I felt sorry for her, but then instantly questioned the sincerity, and even the meaning, of my pity. Did I really think I could understand what kind of struggle was going on in her mind? And if I really felt so sorry for her, why had my answer, the first real words we'd ever spoken, been for the other customers' amusement and not for her consolation?

When I didn't further respond, she looked back to the letter she was writing and I returned to the *New York Review of Books.*

The next time I looked up, when I was ringing up an order for one of the many struggling cartoonists that haunt late-night copy shops all over the country, she was asleep. The cartoonist followed my eyes over to her and then back to mine and he rolled his eyes.

By fall, Myrna was sleeping in the store every night. She no longer made the pretense of making copies and would just come in and write her letters by a computer terminal and then go to sleep. I continued waking her at about six in the morning, when the early morning resumé rush began, and she would gather her stuff, a big red mark on her forehead, and make her way out the door.

Once I had a long conversation about her with one of the Baptist ministers that often came in on Saturday nights copying hymnals for the next day's service. There were several such ministers among the regulars and they were very friendly. I noticed how much more approachable they were than the suburban Catholic priests I had known growing up. They smiled and laughed and seemed to actually be at peace. The priests I knew always seemed so burdened with dogma and propriety, and so remote behind those ridiculous robes. These ministers were real people in real clothes talking a real language. I remember being very impressed by them.

One minister in particular struck me as an eminently decent man. He was short and dressed like inner-city blacks used to on Quinn Martin television shows in the early seventies: big lapels, plush fabrics, sliver of a mustache. He usually came in with a very tall, overly made-up woman and they both laughed and teased each other and then put on a show of flirtation for me at the counter as they paid their bill. This was the one who one night asked me about Myrna. I didn't know her name yet, but I told him she had started coming in about three months ago and that she was there almost every night.

"Doesn't the manager say anything?" he asked, looking over at her with the genuine kind of concern that, I thought, transcends pity. The kind I wished, or sometimes flattered myself, that I had.

"I make her leave before the morning person gets here," I said and shrugged.

He shook his head. "It's getting worse every day."

His tall ladyfriend pouted and leaned against the counter, shaking her head. I nodded and we all looked over at sleeping Myrna.

"Well," he said, putting his wallet back in the breast pocket of his jacket. "Anyway, it's a good thing that you do, letting her sleep in here. I've seen others in here too."

I blushed and looked away.

"It's a good thing."

"Well," I said, uncomfortably, but, I have to admit, glad someone was noticing, "there's really no reason not to."

"Oh," he said, looking at his friend, "there're plenty of reasons not to."

One morning after Myrna left, I noticed one of her letters crumpled up in a garbage can. I pulled it out and read it while I waited for the morning person. It was addressed, strangely, to the editor of the *New York Review of Books* and was about an international ring of child abusers headquartered in Palermo, Italy, that organized staged beatings of children for a vast and secret audience of decadent middle-class Americans who went to great and unspecified lengths to watch a child be mercilessly beaten. She said these events usually took place beneath the bleachers of stadiums during sporting events. These sites were chosen to give cover to the decadent middle-class Americans who attended the beatings, and so the cheers of the crowds would cover the screams of the child.

Myrna then went on to describe one such event that she was at under Cleveland Municipal Stadium. "Mr. Charles Otterheim, III, a wealthy banker, had his son come out onto a semidarkened stage where he caressed his face, paying particular attention to the line of his chin. What little light there was on the stage then faded, leaving only one bare white spot, just barely encircling the frightened child as a recorded symphonic work began to quietly play. Mr. Charles Otterheim, III, had vanished into darkness. Then, as the audience full of decadent middle-class Americans sat in tense and very nearly sexual silence, he began kicking his son. He started with a boot to his groin, which sent a charge through the audience that I cannot describe in a letter to the editor of the *New York Review of Books*.

"Mr. Charles Otterheim, III, continued beating his son with utter disregard for his well-being and to the shuddering delight of the crowd. With each blow the spotlight grew larger and larger and the recorded symphonic work grew louder and louder. Soon the entire stage was brightly lit and you could see the pure, animalistic fury on Mr. Charles Otterheim, III's, face as he kicked and punched the now nearly lifeless form of his son. As the recorded symphonic work reached crescendo, Mr. Charles Otterheim, III, picked up his son by his legs, swung him in a giant arc and in sync with the crash of a gong, smashed his head open on the stage. The performance lasted ten minutes.

"The audience of decadent middle-class Americans then quietly lined up to walk past the mangled body on the stage. Some would kick or perhaps shove it a bit with their feet, and then shake the hand of Mr. Charles Otterheim, III, who was seated in a canvas chair wiping perspiration and splattered drops of his son's blood from his face with a white towel."

Myrna ended her letter with a plea to the editors of the *New York Review of Books* to publicize this tragedy so that others would not have to endure such torture, "and so that the decadence of the American middle class can once and for all be established beyond any shadow of a doubt."

A couple of days later I got my new issue of the *New York Review of Books* and it had a long critique of recovered memory syndrome in it, the first of what was promised to be a three-part essay. I read it at work that night and learned that there was an epidemic of women reporting "recovered memories" of ritualized, satanic abuse they'd suffered as children. Women from all over the industrialized world—Europe, Australia, the U.S., and Canada—were "remembering" in therapy that as children they had witnessed all sorts of unspeakable, staged, ritualized mutilations and murders of children. Some remembered actually participating in murders of infants, stabbing little babies to death in underground satanic chapels lit by candles and filled with their neighbors and families. Many recalled being raped and impregnated by their fathers only to have the resultant infant butchered or eaten or drained of its blood, which was then drunk in a ritualized orgy.

When Myrna came in that night she smiled at me as she took her place at her favorite computer. I had read most of the first part of the article by the time she got in, and despite the writer's attempt to paint this as hysteria, I was nearly pale, imagining the existence of a bizarre, evil world of unknown deeds beginning to show its head for the first time in history.

Late that night a semiregular came in to make copies of a graph. He was a burly guy with a thick mustache who usually came in carrying a big can of imported beer from the deli next door. He also usually wore a medical or lab coat with a stethoscope conspicuously dangling from its side pocket. He always looked hurried, breathed heavily, and ran his fingers through his hair every few seconds.

That night he had trouble with one of the machines that I couldn't fix for him and he threw a minor temper tantrum, something that no matter how regularly it occurred, I never got used to. I just walked away, as blasé as I could, picked up my *New York Review of Books* and resumed reading.

"Well," he shouted. "How are you going to remedy this for me?"

I shrugged and feigned indifference while my heart pounded.

"Excuse me," he shouted, "but, uh, I've got a problem here."

"Well," I said, my chest tightening in rage, "as I explained, I don't know what the problem is." And I went back to reading.

The burly student then came charging over to the counter, he stopped when he saw what I was reading. "Oh, I'm sorry. I didn't realize you were an intellectual. Excuse me for interrupting . . ."

"Look," I said, "I don't have to . . . "

"Yes you most certainly *do* have to. You work—despite whatever lofty ambitions you may have—in a service job, and it is your job to serve the customer—at this moment, me. Now, I want to know your name and the name of the manager at this . . ."

Just then Myrna shouted, "James? James, is that you?"

This distracted us both as Myrna walked over to him and said, "James, what are you doing here?"

"I, um, I don't know you . . . ," he said, clearly upset and distracted. He looked at me for help as Myrna bowed her head and leaned into him, intending to give him a big hug. He jumped back, as though she were a leper.

"James, why did you leave me? I've been all alone."

"Listen," he said, his arms raised in disgusted retreat, "I think, you've got me confused . . ."

Myrna had started crying by this time and was following him as he backed toward a wall. "Why, James, why?"

Finally, he just made a dash around her and ran out the door. Myrna followed him, sobbing and reaching for him as he fled. After he was gone, Myrna turned around, smiled coyly, and walked back to her terminal.

Working the midnight shift I rarely had time to spend with friends, but every now and then I would get together with Gloria, an old college friend who was in town doing an internship at the art museum. She was from a moderately wealthy Pennsylvania steel family that had fallen on what passed for hard times among their class. (She joked that they had to trade the Portuguese villa for a time-share in St. Pete. "Can you imagine," she would say, "a *time-share*. And it's within—brace yourself—*driving distance* of Disneyworld.")

Usually we would get together for coffee and talk about how odd our lives were. Mine, because a bachelor's degree seemed to be doing nothing for me, and hers because she had begun to question whether or not it was moral to have as much money as she had.

"I'm not ready to give anything up," she said one night not long after I'd read Myrna's letter, "let's get that clear right away. And if you quote me on any of this, I'll deny it to the grave. But, my God, by *what right* do we have all of this?" she asked and then made a sweeping motion with her hands, as though implicating all of us.

"I don't have that much," I reminded her.

"You live like a *king*, compared to most of the world. We all do." She sipped her coffee, smiling at her mischief. "Sometimes I think all Americans are going to hell. Irrespective of what we do while we're here. We are marked at birth. It's a lost cause."

"Meanwhile, you drive an Acura."

"Meanwhile—exactly—meanwhile, I drive an Acura. Exactly." She shook her head and then looked down into her mug. "I'm partly serious, you know," she said after a while and I nodded. "I was thinking about the Third World the other day. Just that term: it's like we need to call it that so it seems like it's not real, like it's not even *this* world. But it is. It's the same world we live in. Right now. This world and the Third World are the same world." She pointed across the room. "See those coffee-shop longhairs over there about to favor us with song?" She pointed at the band setting up. "They're in the same world as the people in . . . I don't know, wherever: Kabul. The same world. And so are we."

I said nothing, just nodded.

"I mean, just imagine: If the U.S. government said it would give citizenship to any person and all his family and descendants if he would be willing to, I don't know, give up an arm or a leg—or even his *life*—there'd probably be half a billion people lining up. Just think about that. And what did we do to deserve what we have?"

She looked at me like she really expected an answer. "Nothing?" I guessed, sensing this was where she was going.

"Exactly," she said. "Exactly nothing. We were born. With the kind of advantages people dream about for a lifetime, but will never, ever, ever, *ever* know. And we hoard it. It wouldn't really be so bad if we didn't go to such lengths to keep it all to ourselves."

"It's true," I said, because it is and I couldn't deny it. "I'm not so sure about hell, but I suppose we'll pay somehow."

"I hope it's hell. Fire and brimstone. It'd serve us right." There was a long pause and we both looked around the room. Finally, Gloria smiled and said, "So, enough reality, eh? Let's slip back into sanctioned discourse, you and I. I'll go first. How's the copy shop treating you? Now: Say something banal."

We both laughed, but then I said, "Well, something sort of odd and kind of interesting's been happening there." I told her the whole story about Myrna (I'd learned her name from the letter) and about the international ring of child abusers headquartered in Palermo, Italy, that she wrote to the *New York Review of Books* about. "And," I said, "à la your political bent, she says her mission in writing the letter is to expose the decadence of the American middle class."

"Godspeed to the crazy little lady, I say." I smiled. "You sure meet a crew at that place."

Sipping my coffee, I admired the brightness in Gloria's eyes. Then the band started up and Gloria let out a small scream. "Yikes!" she said. "Let's get out of here," as the band played the first notes of "A Hard Rain's a Gonna Fall."

On our way home, walking across the campus of a small private college, I told Gloria about the article I'd read about ritual satanic abuse.

"Oh yeah," she said, "I've heard about that too. I love that phrase." And she repeated it: "Ritual satanic abuse."

"What do you think?"

"People have too much free time in this country."

"That's all? That's your answer for everything."

"Well, actually, now that you bring it up, I heard a woman on NPR say that her theory was that there was a collective guilt in the Western world about the—she called it the 'casualization'—

of abortion and that it was expressing itself in the female collective unconscious."

"Now *that's* odd."

"You think? Sounded pretty sensible to me. She wasn't one of those wackos. Some kind of a Ph.D. She wasn't blaming abortion, she was blaming the morality trip the wackos put on women who have them. All that baby-killer stuff." She stopped for a second. "Very important distinction."

We were at the front of her building and we both stopped, awkwardly staring at each other. "You know," she said, grinning devilishly, "we could go on up for a sport-fuck if you want."

Gloria and I spent our senior year "sport-fucking" (it was her term), but hadn't since. It had been a bad year for both of us, just recovering from long relationships gone bad.

"Come on," she said. "You were always good . . . for a *guy*."

I laughed, and she grabbed my crotch.

One night I went over to the computer workstation where Myrna was writing and sat down at a nearby computer. I played with Photoshop for a while and then turned to smile at her.

"How are you tonight?" I asked.

"Fine," she nearly shouted. She talked at the same volume as when I was across the room. "I'm trying to put a stop to the Palermo Italians and their international child abuse ring."

I hadn't expected her to jump right into the subject I was interested in, but I was thrilled. "I've heard they have beatings right here in Cleveland," I said.

"Hopkins International Airport is the World Trade Center in child killing and abuse. There's a whole other airport that no one knows about. They ship children in from all over the world in crates and send them out to beatings all over the country."

"So it's not always parents beating their own children."

"No, those are just the hardest to get into."

"How much are the tickets? I'd like to go."

"You don't pay with *money*," she said. "You have to give them something real."

"Money isn't real?"

"Hah! Of course money isn't real," she laughed and shook her head. "Where are you *from*?"

About a month later, my bachelor's degree finally came through and I got a real job. On my second-to-last night at the copy shop, at about three in the morning, I noticed a stream of cars pulling into the parking lot across the street. I thought I recognized a couple of them and then I knew that I did. I went into a mild, paralyzing panic as I saw Mike, the manager, Will, assistant manager, two or three employees, and Jerry, the assistant district sales rep, waving to me through the windows. Mike was holding a bottle of champagne in each hand as he dashed across the street.

Myrna was asleep at her terminal, which was bad enough, but there was a new guy, a real nutcase, sitting in the desktop publishing section, by the *good* computers, smoking cigarettes and muttering to himself. He'd shown up a few nights before, shoeless and filthy, pushing one of those baby strollers yuppies use when they jog with infants. I told him he could spend the night, and he'd come back up every night since.

After a lot of explaining, I managed to convince everyone that I had gone soft on my last week and that this was the first time I'd ever let people sleep or hang out and smoke in the store. The other workers snickered a lot, but the three bosses all looked stern and disappointed. The muttering nutcase left without a problem and then I went to try to wake Myrna. I tapped her shoulder a few times but she wouldn't budge and I shrugged and looked over at Mike, Will, and Jerry. They each had their arms folded across their chests.

"Is this really such a big deal?" I asked.

Will, who seemed to be the most offended, then came stomping toward Myrna and me, saying, "How hard is this?" He pushed me aside and began shaking Myrna until she lifted her head. He helped her up and gathered her things and helped her shove them in her bag and then walked her quickly to the door. He kept calling her Ma'am, saying, "I'm sorry Ma'am, company rules Ma'am. Gotta go, Ma'am." When he got her out the door he turned around and clapped his hands together, grinning like an athlete. "All right," he said, "let's have some bubbly."

No one spoke, and then Will continued, "Look, my first store was in New York, okay? Fact one: people live in the street. Fact two: that's *not* my fault."

I almost didn't come in the next day, but I finally decided I should, in case Myrna showed up. It was probably the busiest night I'd ever spent there. The big copier at the city's other two stores were both broken, so they sent me all their business. I don't think I sat down once all night. Myrna never showed. At dawn, Will came in instead of Julio, who he said had called in sick. As I was packing to leave, he said, "Listen, I wouldn't've cared about that woman if Mike and Jerry weren't there." I saw Mike when I came for my last check and he told me he wouldn't have cared if Will and Jerry hadn't been there. I never saw Jerry.

Within a month at my new job I'd earned enough money to move out of the student housing slum around the copy shop and I got a real apartment with big airy rooms and a little balcony where I could sit in the evenings and listen to music or read a book. I got a dog. Gloria started coming over more and more, scolding me one night after a sport-fuck for coming dangerously close to making love. "A little too much tenderness there, bucko," she said, refastening her bra on the dining room floor.

At the end of her internship she was offered a job at the art museum in the communications department. She took it, she said, "in the absence of the resolve to become a nun or a Red Cross volunteer." I made friends at my job and she made friends at her job and we started going out to concerts and plays in large well-dressed groups, sometimes afterward having dinner in nice restaurants. We rode our mountain bikes through racially integrated residential neighborhoods of seventy-year-old architecturally diverse houses, and shyly pointed to our favorites.

One night, several months into our new lives, as we called them, I had to run a late night errand for her just before having sex. We had a rule where every Friday we would fulfill one of our sexual fantasies. It was her turn and she said she had a doozy but that I would need to get hand lotion and some ice cream at the convenience store around the block, and three carrots. We'd been making out for a long time on the couch and were both half undressed. I pulled myself together while she sat on the couch in her underwear. I took the dog with me to get her late walk over with.

"Chocolate," Gloria shouted across the apartment, as I pulled the door closed. "Häagen Dazs."

On the way back from the store I ran into Myrna. She was sitting on a bench in a small playground on the corner. I hadn't seen her on the way to the store, but Lucy started barking at her as we passed.

"Hello, Poochy!" she shouted, holding out her hand, seemingly unafraid of her snarling.

I yanked her leash and she relaxed. "Myrna?" I said.

She looked up at me and squinted to look into my eyes. "Ha! You," she said. "Ha!"

"Do you remember me?"

She smiled and nodded. "Nice dog."

I'd spent months looking out for her after that last night and was thrilled to see her again. "I'm sorry about that night you got thrown out," I said as Lucy nudged her way to Myrna's outstretched hand.

"If this dog could talk!" she shouted. "Christ. We think animals love us, but they don't. We misinterpret a really quite pathetic obsequiousness for love."

I barely listened to her. "Did you ever go back to the store? Did my replacement let you stay there?"

"She'd probably rip your throat right out if she could. If this was the world *she* wanted. Animals don't live in the world *they* want."

Lucy was eating up the attention, squirming in circles under Myrna's petting. It was starting to get cold—it was early October—and I wondered where she was sleeping. "Do you need a place to stay for the night?" I asked. "Aren't there shelters downtown?"

An empty bus raced past and lightly sprinkled us with water.

"I had a dog once," she said. "Got chopped in half by a harvester."

"Why don't you come to my house for the night. In the morning we can call around and find a place for you. There's got to be a place for you."

"Ha!" she said, finally looking up from the dog. "There's a million places for me. I got a sister."

I thought for some reason that she would argue, would want to stay in the street, but she quickly got her stuff together, lit a cigarette, and stood in front of me, waiting to be led.

The whole way home she told me that the person most people think is Mick Jagger is not in fact Mick Jagger but a Palermo Italian she knew who had stolen his mind. At one point I almost reached out to take her hand before crossing a street.

My apartment was on the third floor of a walk-up and the stairs were hard on her. On the landing after the second flight, she had to stop. She sat down on a stair to rub her leg and pulled up her pants, revealing skin that was badly chapped and swollen. In the light I took a good look at her and saw that she looked much worse than she had at the copy shop. I noticed that her face was chapped too, and was even bleeding in spots.

"You ready?" I asked after a while, feeling slightly anxious and uncertain.

"These legs," she said under her breath, sounding perfectly normal. I think it was the first time I'd heard her speak in less than a shout.

We slowly made our way up the last flight, and as I unlocked the door to my apartment I heard someone running across the floor giggling. Just then I remembered that I had some hand lotion, a carton of ice cream, and three carrots. I pushed the door open and Gloria ran up to me completely naked and was about to jump into my arms when she saw Myrna.

Myrna shouted, "Ha!" and Gloria screamed and ran crouched over herself into the bathroom. "*Hel-lo Cindy,*" Myrna shouted. She put her hand up to her forehead in a mock salute and began marching in place and making fake trumpet noises, as Lucy jumped all over her, thrilled by all the chaos.

I left Myrna in the kitchen to go console Gloria in the bathroom. I found her standing in the bathtub with the water running, rubbing a red Magic Marker target off her belly and thighs. "Jesus Christ," she said, pale and scrubbing harder than she needed to. "Who the hell is that?"

"Her name's Myrna," I said. "She used to sleep in the copy shop. I told you about her . . ."

"What are you going to do with her? Is this something I should know about you? That you sometimes come home with homeless people?"

"Well," I said, "it's not really something . . ."

She stopped scrubbing and looked straight at me. "We were in the middle of something, you know?"

"I forgot," I admitted.

"You *forgot*. Look at me." She spread her arms wide, displaying her body, with the streaking remains of a bull's-eye spread across her belly. I smiled as I wondered what exactly she'd had in mind. Imagining it, I took what must have looked like a predatory step toward her with my arms outstretched. "Oh, no," she said stepping back. "You blew your chance, buddy. Now go fetch my clothes."

I heard her words, and although I knew I should listen to them, reason had vanished and all I saw was a naked body smeared with Magic Marker standing in my bathtub. I grabbed her in our familiar way and, although she put up a front of resistance, before long we were well beyond any hopes of stopping. I had to stifle her yelps with a powder-blue hand towel she'd bought me a few weeks before.

Afterward, Gloria told me it was too bad I'd have to wait two weeks to find out what the carrots were for. She brushed her teeth and then put her ear to the door as I pulled my clothes back on. She turned back to me and held her nose, "My god," she said. "Do you know I can smell her in here?"

"She was a regular," I said, creeping up behind her for final inventory of pats and squeezes. "What could I do? It's like we were friends."

She slapped my hands away and then turned around for a final, long kiss. "Don't forget to put the ice cream away," she said as I left.

We decided to leave the bathroom one at a time. I went and collected Gloria's clothes and then joined Myrna in the kitchen, where she was sitting on the floor scratching Lucy's snout. As I walked in she was telling her that "liberation is not far off."

"She doesn't want to be liberated," I said. "She's very happy."

Myrna slowly stood up, supporting herself between the cabinets and the table, and said, "That's just a convenient thought. I don't blame you. We'd all commit suicide without convenient thoughts."

Eventually, Gloria joined us, bundled in a bathrobe, and we all sat at the kitchen table eating ice cream while Myrna told us about "a conspiracy of toddlers," which she said was "reducing public debate to goo-goos and ga-gas."

In the morning Gloria and I drove Myrna to a shelter and shook hands with her when we left. On the ride home Gloria rolled down her window and took a deep breath of the cool autumn air. The sun was bright and we both wore dark glasses. "She lives in another world," I said, and then neither of us spoke for a minute.

"When I was teenager," Gloria finally said, "I used to pray a UFO would come down and abduct me and I could go to their planet and be a huge celebrity. 'The Earthling!' I'd travel all over and all the aliens would be amazed by me."

"Me, too."

"Really?" she said and I nodded. "Good." She stuck her arm out the window and let the wind blow it up and down, using her hand as a wing. She sunk down into her seat and turned the radio up. It was tuned to a Saturday morning bluegrass show we always listened to. "I'm still waiting."

"Me, too." After a minute or two of shrill, wild banjos, I added, "Of course, what would really happen is they'd torture you with experiments, keep you in a cage for a couple of years and then do a globally televised autopsy."

"Thank you, Mr. Realism," she said, sounding actually irritated. "Thank you, Mr. Can't Let a Girl Have a Dream."

Two summers later, Gloria said it was time to acknowledge that the sport had left our fucking, that we'd sloppily let ourselves start making love and that the only sensible thing to do was to get married. She took me to Pittsburgh for a week and we stayed in the stone mansion (actually *on* a hill) that she grew up in. I met all her relatives and her mother planned a skiing honeymoon in Chile. I played tennis with her brother Brian on a beautiful clay court behind the house and let him beat me while Gloria watched.

On our last night in Pittsburgh her mother and father relented and let us sleep in the same room. It was in a section of the house nobody really spent that much time in. At dusk we explored its many darkened rooms and fooled around a little in several of them. Late that night we were lying in each other's arms and she said, "You let Brian beat you, didn't you?" The question sparked memories of Myrna. I laughed and reminded Gloria of the night she spent in my old apartment.

"Do you remember," I asked, "when I told you about how she used to talk about an international ring of child abusers headquartered in—what was it?—somewhere in Italy, that fed off the decadence of the American middle class? Palermo. The Palermo Italians."

"Oh, yeah," she said. "That was during my 'We're All Going to Hell' phase right?"

"Yeah," I said, laughing at the memory. It had been quite a while since I'd heard her curse our fates.

"Yeah," she said, "I remember. We were at that horrible coffee shop. And then we talked about ritual satanic abuse—God, I love that phrase." She sat up and repeated it. "Ritual satanic abuse." She laughed and then fell back into my arms. "What a strange time. I wonder what ever happened to all your little street people."

I instantly tensed, and craned my neck to look down at Gloria cuddling up with me. As she was burrowing down to get more comfortable she suddenly stopped and sat back up.

"My god, listen to me: 'your little street people.' Did I really say that?" She looked at me and pushed a strand of hair out of her eyes. "We really are all going to hell, aren't we?"

"My guess is yes," I said, half kidding, and she collapsed back onto the bed.

The Prodigal Corpse

My father's corpse sat smiling at the kitchen table. He was perspiring and out of breath, tearing at a hunk of dark bread with his teeth. His skin was rotten from having been buried for nearly two weeks. We were all astonished to see him and sat nervously waiting for him to finish his bread. Mother had drawn the curtains.

The three-piece suit we had buried him in hung on him in rags. The trousers were tattered and were suspended with a rugged piece of twine. Somewhere along the journey home his jacket had been discarded and he wore only the suit's smart blue vest. His shoes were ripped and muddy and showed decaying, nailless toes. In life, he had preferred the three-piece suit—so popular, it seems, in real estate (where he, in fact, spent most of his professional life following in his father's footsteps), and his vests were for some reason always bunching up on him at the belly, making him look stout in a way he really wasn't. Beyond that, however, he had always looked miserably uncomfortable in them, nervously pacing the early-morning house like an overweight stray.

In the ragged remainder of his favorite blue suit, however, he looked happier than I think I'd ever seen him. He seemed to be reveling in our confusion and horror. He'd tear at the bread in big chunks, chew vigorously—with his mouth wide, something that, again, wasn't his habit in life—and look around at all our horrified faces. He'd wink and grin and laugh, barely able, at times, to remain seated. He seemed free, whereas in life he'd always seemed tormented in a way that was infectious, so that just to be around him was, sad to say, unpleasant.

Suddenly he stopped. His face grew serious. He leaned silently across the table. We all bent cautiously toward him. He motioned that we move even closer. Our chairs squeaked as they scraped across the floor, our breaths drawn and held nervously. We huddled. He looked at all of us—turning methodically from sallow face to sallow face. His eyes were grim and vacant, his breath came in studied intervals and held us in near trance. Then, suddenly, just when we could stand the tension no more he jumped out of his chair and shouted, "BOOOO!!!" and then fell back laughing in huge animated guffaws, patting his quivering belly.

Mother nearly fainted. My sister ran screaming from the room. My heart pounded relentlessly and I felt a slight moisture grow between my legs.

A few minutes later my sister returned from vomiting in the upstairs bathroom. I'd changed my pants and brought mother an iced tea and a cold compress. Father stood at the sink rinsing his dishes under steaming water while whistling a patriotic tune. I held Mother's hand in mine until he finished. He held our attention masterfully, I noticed. A strange quiet clamped us around him. We sat hungrily awaiting his every move, his every word and gesture. He shut off the water, holding a goblet of sparkling crystal upside down at eye level, as the last drops of soap fell from it in tiny bubbles into the sink. "Beautiful," he observed as they dropped, tilting his head to one side, "stunning."

Returning to the table he told us the remarkable story of his escape from the coffin we'd buried him in. It was a very difficult procedure, it seems, mostly due to the fact that he had no tools other than his bare hands, and it took quite some time. Even though, his tone was pleasant and he told his tale with gaiety and in a lively, engaged manner that nearly allowed you to forget the grisly subject. He seemed happy to be finally back among us, and, in a most unsettling way, absolutely unaware of just how remarkable that in itself truly was.

By mid-afternoon, he had grown tired of his tale and begged off to catch what he cacklingly described as "a little shut-eye."

The rest of the day passed without incident. Mother, my sister, and I said practically nothing about his return. At one point I was playing cards with my sister while Mother was doing the dishes, and I thought I heard her mutter, "strangest thing," over the running water. Then, later, as we all watched television in the darkened living room with Mother folding freshly washed linens on the empty love seat, she said—although I don't think it was spoken to us in particular—"I suppose he's back then."

I barely slept at all that night and when I did it was fitfully. I tossed about a great deal and at one point got so angry at my inability to sleep I started punching my pillow with all my might. I must've made quite a racket for my sister hushed me from across the hall.

I kept thinking of Mother. What a thing to have happen! I wondered where she would sleep. The smell of him was, to be blunt, overpowering even from a polite distance—but to have to sleep with him! Well, it was unthinkable. And it didn't strike me as the sort of odor that washes away with a good scrubbing either.

I was relieved to find the next morning Mother asleep on the downstairs couch. It was still very early and the sun had not yet risen. I'd gotten up to shake off the horror I was feeling as the result of a dream I'd had. It was a gritty and brutally realistic dream very unlike the fantastic sort of fairy-filled ones in which I usually passed my nights. It involved a bloody murder accomplished with my compliance and perhaps participation. The degree of my guilt was confoundingly oblique and led to a lengthy criminal procedure that captured the nation's attention.

I rose to calm my nerves and my stomach with a snack.

"I'm awake," Mother whispered from the couch as I tried to sneak past her into the kitchen.

I stopped to look down at her. I could only barely make her out in the predawn darkness. It appeared she had her favorite afghan pulled snugly up under her chin.

"This is not supposed to happen," she said. I dropped to my knees and held out a hand to hers. I took her soft, frail hand in mine and brought it to my lips. I knelt there beside her as a series of soft, pained sighs emanated from her. I sat with her, next to the couch, holding her hand in mine, until the sun slowly illuminated the second day of Father's return. In the light, bravery returned and Mother rose with a sigh, tossed her afghan aside and walked out of the room, barely taking note of me as she said, in a resigned tone, "Well, I must see what's to be done." I crouched still at the side of the couch and I listened as her footsteps plodded heavily, dutifully up the steps.

Father was up shortly after that. He looked rested, rubbing his hands together as he walked into the kitchen with a hearty smile. He was dressed exactly as he had been the day before. His hair, still as thick and curly as it had been in life, was a mess, practically standing on end.

"Beautiful morning!" he cheered and sat heavily into his chair. "I'll just have some coffee."

I made him his coffee as was my custom before his death and brought it to him in his favorite mug. "Boy," he said, "that sure smells good." And he held it under what was left of his nose and inhaled deeply.

I joined him at the table awkwardly, unsure of my welcome. He looked out the window at the big empty field behind the house, a calm, serene smile across his badly decomposed face. I noticed he held himself in a confident way such as he never did while living. In life, he'd been rather withdrawn and cautious, both unsettling and unsettled. He never seemed to know quite what to do with himself, as if his very existence were conditional upon someone else's approval. I wondered about this change in him—as he slurped his coffee—wondered what might have brought it on.

"Death'll do it to you," he said, as though in answer to my thoughts and turning suddenly to face me. "It'll change a man like practically nothing else can." He stared at me as his words sunk in. He appeared briefly thoughtful, looked into his steaming mug, and then nodded to me as though he were about to impart a secret. "Let me tell you a few things about dying," he said, smiling slyly, "just between you and me and the radiator [This was an odd turn of phrase, in that we had always lived in houses with forced air heat]. The biggest is that there's nothing to it. It's the easiest thing in the world. Gives you a whole new perspective on the foolishness that preceded it. That's what you realize when you're sitting there waiting to go, when you know it's really coming, with that just-before-the-roller-coaster-drop sinking feeling in your gut, you realize, hey, what do I got to be afraid of? I've been *alive* for crying out loud. What can death be that's worse than cold-call selling, than signing a thirty-year mortgage at the age of twenty-four, than sitting in a foxhole in Korea." His tone turned dark and he lowered his mug to the table with a studied intensity. "Than Disneyworld in August with two ungrateful kids." He leaned forward across the table until his face was just inches from my own. "Or a twenty-year marriage to a woman afraid of the *word* 'penis.'"

I swallowed hard and tried not to look away as sweat formed all over my body.

"Penis," he said quietly and leaned back in his chair. "Penis," he said and cocked his head to one side, a slight smile breaking across his face. "Did someone say penis? Penis?" He stood up and began prancing about the room assuming the posture and personage of various absurd caricatures. "Is that you penis? Well, hello, penis, I'd like to introduce you to cock. Have you met? No? Well, you'll find you have a world in common. And wait till you make schlong's acquaintance, and pecker over there, you'll get a real bang out of him." He opened one of the kitchen cabinets and pulled out Mother's best stew-kettle and took her decorative brass ladle from its mooring above the stove and began banging one into the other and shouting at the top of his lungs, "Penis penis penis penis penis!!!!!!"

The racket was deafening and brought Mother and my sister running down the stairs in tears. My sister flung her arms around my waist and collapsed to her knees with her head in my lap as Mother dug her nails into my shoulder, biting savagely into the knuckles of her other hand as we all stared at Father's corpse march in place while banging ladle to kettle and screaming "penis" at the top of his lungs.

Finally he was finished and he turned to face us. "God," he said, calmly, "that was fun. You want to try, dear?" He picked up the kettle and held it out to her, mocking her savagely. "Vagina vagina vagina," he whispered as he carried it over to the bunch of us. "That's really nowhere near as fun. How about this: Pussy pussy pussy." He smiled broadly and continued his approach. "That's the one." He made kissing sounds as he approached us, "here pussy-pussy," he whispered. "Here pussy-pussy."

The kettle dropped at our feet and Father stood staring intensely at us. I could feel my sister's heart pounding, my shoulder going numb from Mother's terrified clutch. The horror and the taunting's zenith having been achieved, Father suddenly broke his stare, stood straight up, spread a wide grin across his face and said, curiously, "Anyone feel like a quick eighteen holes?"

The rest of the morning the house was filled with music as Father played the stereo and polished his old set of golf clubs, which he'd dragged from the basement. At first he was listening to old easy-listening albums and certain jazz singers from the 1950s. But then toward noon he launched into early rock and roll, especially the Beatles. He moved the best stereo in the house, the one in my sister's room, into the living room and had wires running all over as he played one album after another, gaily singing along as he polished club after club. He shook his head and screamed and shouted along with the music, sometimes holding a club as though it were an electric guitar. When he noticed me watching him from the kitchen, he turned the stereo down, picked up a pitching wedge and said, "If there's any sense to be made of life—and I'm not saying there is—I'm pretty sure it has something to do with hitting a three-wood on a hot summer morning down a perfectly trimmed fairway." He then mimed just such a stroke, in dramatic slow motion, pretending even to shield his eyes from the morning sun as he watched his imaginary ball soar. Then he flashed me a smile, turned the music back up and wiggled his backside.

That evening as the sun descended, with the music still howling from the living room, I found myself drawn into my sister's room. A few minutes before, I'd gone downstairs and found Father practicing his putting. His skin appeared to be in pretty bad shape. Much worse than it had looked that morning during his tirade of the unmentionables. I don't think he noticed me and I left quickly.

My sister was sitting quietly on her meticulously made bed, a soft, pink throw-pillow clutched tightly across her chest. She was staring at the wall with an utterly blank expression on her face. I came in and collapsed on the bed with her.

"What are we supposed to do?" she asked.

My bewilderment left me dumb.

"Evelyn's supposed to sleep over tonight."

My heart raced. I had nearly forgotten the world outside.

Mother came in shortly after. Of all of us, this had been the hardest on her. You could see it in her eyes. She looked exhausted, frightened, vacant. She'd become, over the last day and a half, fidgety. She hadn't slept at all—could hardly in fact keep still, especially since the morning's outburst of foulness. She bit her nails and tossed her hands up in the air. She really was lost as to what was expected of her. Everything had always been so clear for her. She married young—moved right from her mother's house into her husband's. She was taken care of nicely by both. She never required an income of her own or wanted for anything and then, suddenly, her husband was dead, and then, remarkably, this latest twist.

I feared for her well-being.

Mother paced back and forth at the foot of the bed. At times she would stop suddenly and turn, as though near speech, but then she would fade, deflate, and start pacing again.

When she finally spoke, it was a single word: "How?"

I instinctually moved over on the bed and Mother fell into its soft pinkness with my sister and me, her head at our feet. She curled up into a ball and began caressing a bed post. "How?" she said again.

Soon, she was sobbing softly as the music downstairs suddenly died. The sound of an ice-cream truck making the rounds of the neighborhood could faintly be heard out the window, as a soft breeze ruffled its pink curtain. My sister said, "Ohh, what I wouldn't do for an ice-cream sandwich." She spoke in a voice so dreamy you would think she was asking for hair of spun gold or a kingdom by the sea.

There were no more sounds from downstairs and I sensed Mother was falling asleep. Her breath was being drawn more regularly and once or twice her leg twitched rapidly. Then my sister fell asleep, her head falling to my shoulder. Before I knew it I, too, had fallen asleep.

It was dark when I awoke. A cold wind was blowing my sister's drapes in a chilling silence. As I gathered my senses I noticed Mother had gone. I softly and quietly made my way from my sister's bed—so as not to awaken her—and began searching the darkened house. I felt something odd in the air, something besides the dampness of an approaching storm that was thick in the night. In the hallway outside Mother's room—what had been her and Father's room—I heard what sounded like a whispered argument interspersed with grunts and groans. There was a mild scream, the sound of flesh slapping flesh.

As I peered into her (their) room, I tried to prepare myself for whatever it was I would see, but there is no way I could have. Mother was fastened to the bed with colorful polyester ties and faux leather belts. A scarf she was particularly fond of hid her eyes. Her dress had been sliced open up the middle with a pair of scissors I noticed glistening in the moonlight on the bed table.

Father held himself above her with his nearly meatless arms and had (somehow) aroused her into a drooling frenzy in which she was begging him for his thing, using all the words he had tormented her with earlier. After each unrepeatable word he would gently—but with unmistakable masculinity—slap her cheek or her hips and say, "There you go, how hard was that?"

I held my breath. I felt a sickness inside myself, a nausea for our depraved condition. I left the darkened doorway and thought briefly of returning to my sister's bed but instead found solace in the stark emptiness of my own.

When I next awoke, Father was gone. Mother was bruised and though I at first attempted to comfort her, she held me at bay with a telling blush and a wave of her hand. Over time, I noticed she had taken on some of the carefree mannerisms of Father's returned corpse—especially the way she would deeply draw in her breath, smiling at the sensation.

Observer Status

Dad is in the kitchen trying to tie a fishing lure. He has a look of deep concentration on his otherwise likable face. (I notice a cramp growing in my leg and consider pounding it with my fist.) He has a big glossy book open on the table in front of him. It is an illustrated guide to tying fishing lures, published by a relatively minor pretender to the Time/Life throne of how-to manuals.

Big color pictures, happy men in waders.

The next day he will go on a fishing trip with some big shots from his office whom he has misled about his knowledge of hand-tied fishing lures. The day of the misleading he came home saying that his life was a Jerry Lewis movie, which I took to be a reference to its bumbling, rather out-of-control nature; the way in which an existential slapstick at his expense has been the dominant theme of late.

He is at the kitchen table. Behind him the sun is setting through our trees. (Note: Cease describing nature. Irrelevant. Boring.)

We both hear Mom coming before she gets there because she is singing to herself. Dad loosens, wiggles his shoulders free of intensity and:

1) pretends to be enjoying himself;

2) manipulates his body language to relay a sense of ease;

3) attempts to radiate a healthy, comic realization that trying to impress these big shots is silly in a way he *fully recognizes.*

Mom immediately senses the gravity of what is happening at the kitchen table. It hits her like a pie in the face—no, like a blast of unpleasant wind—and in an act of pure charity she calls attention to exactly none of her husband's delusions.

Still, he blushes.

"Figure it out yet?" Mom asks as she glides past him, as usual the first to regain composure, stuffing a carrot stick in her mouth. She had been singing "Don't You Want Somebody to Love?" and has skillfully incorporated the carefree timbre of the song into her gait.

Dad laughs and blushes, again. "Hah," he says, "these stupid things. Can you believe people tie their own fly-fishing lures." He then chuckles some more—unconvincingly, it must be said—and mom stuffs a carrot stick by his mouth while at the same time leaning over to kiss him, creating a traffic jam of options. Dad first leans forward with his mouth open to bite the carrot stick, it being the first proffered, but then thinks better of it and moves toward Mom's lips, which by this time have been pulled away. Dad is left frustrated and sighing as Mom briskly pulls herself together, snickering, "The American Sportsman," as she sweeps herself out of the room.

Mom is beautiful and in this way is exceptional for the moms in my extended circle of mothered friends. Many moms are frumpy, doltish, slow, mean. Many more are single, bitter, overly made-up, energyless. I watch them all parading their broods behind them to school in the morning, pausing at intersections, checking their watches. My mom is beautiful and admired. I have been asked many times by friends if my mom would breast-feed them. I have heard many descriptions of dully imagined sexual experiments my essentially penisless friends would like to perform on her. I never respond to such foolishness; rather I absorb the ambiance of the moment.

This is good, I think. This is *useful.*

Dad goes back to tying his lure. I move a little bit because my back is starting to hurt from crouching behind the couch. I have been observing things—from a variety of positions throughout the house—for two and three-quarter hours. I have hung from curtain rods, peered up from cracks in the floor, imagined whole worlds from nests you wouldn't believe. I dash to my room and begin to write.

To write!

My sister is strolling through the woods with a boy. His name is Jenkins, William, and goes by the name of "Billy." He is easily the toughest kid in school. My sister, foolishly, is trying to interest Billy in trees, the central passion of her life. Billy is looking bored and is trying to divert my sister into thinking about something else. I can almost smell his brain churning, trying to come up with a way to appear playful in a vaguely sexual way, a way that will not offend my sister who is easily the prettiest girl in school but who is known to be bored with the antics of her peers, especially their bumbling, premasculine sexualities, the collective shallowness of which deeply offends her. In household discussions she routinely compares boys her age to Jell-O; to soggy matchbooks; to balding tires. "Things whose existence is, obviously, *empirically evident,* but whose usefulness . . . well, you get my point."

Similar to the discussions I have had with my friends about my mom, so have I had them about my sister. I have had many scenarios described at great length detailing fantastical and generally sadomasochistic antics almost no one would conceivably derive the slightest pleasure from, except of course for the pleasure and psychological coddling implicit in creating them as fantasies and the dumb reassurances they elicit from the cowering batch of peers who backslap the dreamer into a smug sexual security so that he may turn into a productive and healthy heterosexual breeding primate.

We are at the farthest end of the sloping ravine and Billy has made his move. With one hand he grabs my sister at her lower back, a point of high interest in much of what I described above, and with the other he encircles her shoulders, pulling her to him. My sister, as I certainly could have predicted, does nothing except that she stiffens her body like a tree and stands perfectly still as Billy rubs her furiously in a sickening and comic display. Finally, Billy stops and pulls away, releasing my sister as he stomps his feet and shoves his hands into his pockets. My sister says, "Are you quite finished with that childish display?" To which Billy of course does not respond, the answer so obviously being yes, whether he is capable of admitting it or not.

Dad returns from the fishing trip with the big shots from his office with a bright red face and neck. Mom greets him at the door and laughs at him as he slowly and with great discomfort peels off his shirt, grimacing in pain. The whole rest of his body is shockingly white and the contrast has a surreal effect, as if somebody has painted his neck and face the color of an apple laced with alar. "Hah, hah," Dad says as Mom bends over herself in the foyer, laughing till she is forced by the peculiar architecture of the female anatomy to sit. She says: "You truly are becoming Jerry Lewis." Dad then dumps a vase of plastic roses on her head, which makes her laugh even harder and she runs into the bathroom.

Mom and Dad meet in the living room while Dad applies cold cream to his badly burned skin. I can only hear them and any visual embellishment I might add here would be purely speculative, and so, highly suspect, and since my energy is low I won't bother. Mom says: "What happened?" Dad says: "We ended up going out on Allens' boat." Mom says: "My poor sailor." Dad says: "Please." Mom says, after sounds of kissing: "Does that hurt?" Dad says, simultaneously: "Ouch!" Mom says: "How was it, seriously?"

Dad says: "I don't know. I think sometimes the whole world knows something I don't. I mean I sat there on that boat all day, watching everyone play this game, this elaborate game that they all seemed to know the rules to. And they play with such ease. If it wasn't so pathetic, it would've been interesting. I might've learned something. But I just sat there like a mute. Holliman was sucking up to Allens with total abandon. Absolutely shamelessly." Mom says: "What does shame have to do with it?" Dad says: "Bad choice of words." Mom says: "*Revealing* choice of words." Dad says: "Unselfconsciously then. How do people act so unselfconsciously?" Mom says: "My anthropologist (kissing); my confused anthropologist. The ritual is not as complicated as you imagine it." Dad says: "What does everyone know that I don't?" Mom says: "To wear sunscreen on a boat, for one."

I have cut school and watch my mom through the spotted windows of our house all day long. She sent me off to school in the morning but after she closed the doors I doubled back and hid in the large bushes just to the east of our front porch. After drinking her coffee standing up at the kitchen table while flipping through the *Wall Street Journal* with near violence, she goes to her office and begins calling people up. After several calls she turns on her computer and begins keyboarding with scattered incidents of mouseplay. She then gets a phone call and while speaking to Caller Unknown, she rolls up her shirt just slightly in front and examines her belly.

She then spins around in her chair and begins rummaging through her desk finally pulling out (with a look of utter victory) a pair of tweezers. Although she is still engaged in the phone conversation she pulls the phone just slightly away from her mouth, spinning it up and away while keeping the earpiece held firmly to her ear, and rerolls up her shirt to reexpose her belly. She takes the tweezers and grabs a hair in her belly, which she then yanks out, mouthing the word "Yow!" as she does. She returns the mouthpiece to her mouth and resumes conversation with Caller Unknown, at times smiling and at times examining sheets of paper, with a pencil sticking in her hair.

She has an avocado sandwich for lunch in front of the television, flipping channels and moving her long hair into different formations using various ties and clips and then modeling these formations very dramatically in the reflection of the sliding glass doors. In between poses she takes bites of her sandwich, which strikes me as terribly unhygenic but revealing of her arrogant yet endearing untroubledness with the grimier aspects of life.

At the required hour I pretend to come home from school and she hugs me at the door, as is our custom, and rubs my head, so low at her hip, as she leads me into the kitchen where she has carefully laid out an after-school treat that I only minutes ago watched her absently prepare. "We don't see much of our mystery man these days," she says. "We love him very much though," she says and returns to her office.

Dad comes home later than usual and Mom greets him at the front door with her hands on her hips pretending to cry dramatically, saying, "Who is she, who is she?" and then she laughs. Dad throws his jacket over her head as though she were a coatrack and pats her on the behind with his rolled-up newspaper as he yawns past her.

It is a flawless, impromptu performance, a rare feat for Dad who is at times very nearly mystified into a wallowing, dumb inaction by the free-spiritedness of his wife's antics.

Mom rebounds brilliantly, jumping onto his back as they both go bounding into the living room where they begin dancing to unheard music, as if in celebration of the perfection of the performance they have just pulled off; so brilliantly timed and played.

Dinner: my sister tells the story of two boys caught making out in the bathroom and all day everyone was throwing stuff at them and punching them, and how a teacher made a remark about filth and disease in the middle of a class. Mom drops her fork, obviously affected, appalled. She asks if what she has just said is true, the part about the teacher she means and my sister says yes, she was there, right there, heard it with her own ears. It was during civics class. Mom vows to write to the principal and my sister begs her not to. Dad at this point tones in saying that he too will write a letter.

A pall descends.

"As if everything's not hard enough for a kid," Mom says, her voice quaking, visibly upset. Her eyes are pleading, going from face to face looking for an explanation in one of them. "I cannot believe this world," she says and starts crying and then Dad and her leave the kitchen. My sister and I shrug at each other and resume eating. Moments later she says, "Just so you don't grow up warped—or any more so than you already are—I want you to know that being *that* sensitive is *not* a requirement." And she shakes her head. She then says, "The world is full of injustices *so beyond* what I've just described . . ." And she shakes her head. She then says, "Pick your battles, that's what I say." And she shakes her head. She then says, "We are not impressed." And she shakes her head.

It is after dinner and Dad has come into the kitchen, alone, where he sits reading the newspaper without interest. He flips from page to page apparently not reading anything and every few seconds he looks at his watch. He clears his throat, peers around a corner. He closes the newspaper and folds it in half. He flips it over. He pulls out the middle section, opens it, closes it. Soon my sister joins him, sitting down opposite him, and begins filing her nails, something she rarely does. There is a long and strange silence in which their eyes occasionally meet, and during those few seconds odd, meaningless smiles spread across their anxious faces. Finally my sister speaks. "Dad," she says, "would you be mad at me if I decided to have a baby?"

Dad does a double take at this news: a perfectly natural stunned look of panic combined with paralysis and inaction careens—absolutely flies—across his face, and is then wiped clean, only to be instantly beset with the exact same look a microsecond later. It is a thrilling moment of genuine shock, a glimpse that is rarely this purely and truly observed. I feel a warm glow inside.

This is good, I think. This is *useful.*

My sister continues. "I think I would like to be artificially inseminated by a Nobel laureate." My sister stands and takes a deep breath. "I know this is difficult to comprehend from within the cultural morass, so if you could please just take a second and try to free yourself from the stifling limits of this idiotic society with its servile, unimaginative mores, I think you may find my reasoning sound."

She takes a breath and then sits down. She reaches across the table to take Dad's pale and lifeless hand into her own. "Are you free yet?" she says but he does not answer. "I'll just go ahead anyway."

She sits back and clears her throat. "I feel this is a good time to bear children because I am young, school is so ridiculously easy that to call it 'easy,' with the implication inherent in the word that any effort *at all,* however small, is required, is an overstatement of the case, and I have plenty of time. None of these will be the case once I am out of high school. None."

Mom has arrived because Dad pulled himself together enough to call out for her. She is pale and concerned, her eyes sprung wide open. She can barely contain herself, barely sit still. She goes to the refrigerator and pulls out a jar of herring in creme sauce, stopping to grab a handful of spoons before returning to the kitchen table. She picks up the newspaper and folds and refolds it, unable ultimately to get it back into its original shape. She folds it against her womb, her knee, her hip, until it is misshapen and tiny. She sits at the kitchen table wiping ink from her fingertips and spins open the herring in creme sauce.

My sister sighs, arms folded, and she half turns away. "I can see you two are having trouble freeing yourselves from the confines of this idiotic cultural . . ."

"Don't tell me about culture, young lady," Mom warns, wagging a spoonful of herring in the air. "Cultural abstractions have *no place* at this table."

"Oh! Is that so? Well let me tell you something, cultural abstractions abound! To label them ubiquitous would be a comic understatement. They are at the heart of all morality, all judgment—everything!"

"Well, yes," Mom says, leaning forward in battle, "but *only* as abstractions. Abstractions are meaningless when applied to individuals—you know that."

"So, are you really going to stand there and acknowledge the existence of a stifling cultural narrative and then insist that it has no impact on the individual—in this conversation, that would be you two?"

Mom screams a stifled scream in a way that suggests she can barely contain herself. Her eyes and those of my sister are engaged in a silent and, it occurs to me, uniquely feminine battle. I notice Dad has recused himself and the color has returned to his face.

"I know from previous discussions and old photographs depicting a certain social movement the two of you heartily participated in—the costumes and music of which, by the way, have discredited the left for perhaps the next several generations—that you have—or had—a healthy contempt for the wholly arbitrary guiding principles of this empty society. What has happened to that?"

Mom appears near speech, but stops herself, returning to the consolation of a spoonful of herring.

"Listen," my sister says, deflating in a conciliatory way. "Forget that. That was unfair, I know. There is only a small vanguard capable of carrying youthful vision through their twenties, and many of them have trust funds. But hear this: I'll be eighteen soon and will almost certainly earn a full scholarship and then I will be free to do as I please, and believe me, I will do as I please. So if you can't rip yourselves away from the illusion of normalcy you're wallowing in, and you're against it, just say so and I'll wait."

"We're against it," Mom says, lifting a spoonful of herring to her mouth. "We are definitely against it."

My sister shrugs and jams her open palms onto her hips. She looks the two of them in the face and shakes her head in disappointment and says, "At what age should I expect everything to take on such *dramatic meaning*?" She leaves, however, before either can answer, humming.

Mom and Dad are left alone at the table. They each stare at their own private emptiness, seemingly unaware of the other's presence. Mom digs into her herring and well-paced spoonfuls of the North Atlantic white fish climb effortlessly through space to her mouth—one and another and another. The phone rings once and stops.

"Nobel laureates?" Dad asks.

"At least we know she's concerned about genes," Mom says, worried, plaintive, weak, sorrowful. She finishes the jar of herring, holds it up to examine its emptiness, and then drops her spoon. "I wish she would stop deconstructing like that. I just don't have the energy anymore."

Later I sneak downstairs as Mom and Dad sit in a darkened living room with the television on while they make out on the couch. I am at times embarrassed by their childish affection, but more often I am intrigued by the ends to which it drives them, and, it must be said, all adults—with perhaps the exception of my sister, who obviously is not yet fully formed, but has resisted so far the banal animalism of hormonal solicitude. I have heard her describe the sexuality of her peers as "horrific in its drive, amusing in its sloppiness, and uninspired in its jargon."

Mom and Dad, meanwhile, are beginning to slurp and groan on the couch. I look away at one point as Mom sits up to liberate her breasts for Dad's pagan worship ritual. I have seen many similar encounters between the two of them and can only hope that in the impending future the chemicals that drive them to such actions will be depleted. Mom, however, has recently purchased several books on postmenopausal sexuality, and so I'm afraid the two of them will, like many of their peers, continue in this behavior well beyond its naturally productive period.

It's all so embarrassing and leads me to sometimes wonder about the usefulness of these reports. When they finally finish, Mom sits up and refastens her breasts to the elaborate black garment in which they live, suggesting playfully that, despite their shape, they are not honeydew and should therefore not be chewed. She then falls into his arms and begins discussing my sister's unique perspectives on reproduction.

"What was that about?" Dad asks, reaching for an apple from the coffee table bowl.

"Hormones," Mom correctly observes. "She'll be essentially insane for the next five or six years unless we send her off to Switzerland and have her shot full of testosterone to sort of neutralize her."

"What about what she said about us? About how we used to think differently?"

Mom scoffs, waves her hand across the area just in front of her face, looks away, scoffs again, and takes the apple from my father. "She's just being snotty. She thinks we're vulnerable there."

"Aren't we?" Dad asks.

"Don't say 'we,'" Mom says, something she tells him often. "'We' don't exist in that way. 'I'm' not vulnerable. My peace was won long ago."

A long moment of silence follows and I begin to tire. I turn my head and look out the kitchen's bay window into the darkened night. The click of the television going dark catches my attention and they begin sighingly pulling themselves together for the ascent, always with bent backs and heavy feet, to their bedroom.

Reluctantly attended school today and was instructed that our nation was founded by aboriginal European religious fanatics whose harsh ways were not tolerated in their homeland. Little mention of the pregenocide savages that prowled the eastern woodlands. Mr. Glass, the gym teacher, did his best to instill in us a sense of competition, team loyalty, and selflessness. Lawrence, Andy, wasn't sufficiently compliant (he shot distracted layups) and was ritually humiliated.

Socialization continues apace and almost nothing could interest me less.

At home I dodge suspicious glances, the probing eyes of adulthood. Dad is home early from his office, having concocted an attack of diarrhea. He languishes in Mom's office, reading issue after issue of *Computer Graphics Magazine*, shifting, casting distant, needy glances at Mom as she takes calls, manipulates text, imports images, and taps herself on the forehead with the eraser of her favorite pencil.

Finally Dad speaks. He rises from the couch in an awkward

motion and calls Mom "Joan" in a voice that perfectly embodies his peculiar blend of insecurity and unaffected bewilderment at the degree to which his perceptions, concerns, and problems are not as utterly fascinating to those around him as they are to himself.

"Joan," he says, letting the magazine fall and then skid across several others on the coffee table. "I quit my job today."

Mom says nothing. She is sitting in her chair with her lips pursed and her head-tapping pencil held straight in the air, a gnawed yellow obelisk.

I have to concentrate on remaining still. My position is fairly secure and normally I wouldn't worry about being discovered, but this, I can tell, will be a revealing observation.

Breathe deep, remain absolutely still.

"I'm sorry," Mom says, finally returning to animation, "did you say you quit your job?"

Dad rises and pushes his hand through his hair. "I can't do it, Joan. I just can't do it anymore. The stupidity . . . the politics . . ." He looks down at his feet and dramatically, pleadingly points to his shoes. "The shoes. Look at these shoes I'm wearing! My god, I'm a caricature of my worst nightmare."

"You lost me there, Norm. A caricature of a nightmare? Isn't that a bit severe? Assuming of course, I follow you."

Mom has already gained the upper hand in that she has remained seated, calm, and in character. Dad has fallen out of character in a silent appeal that she do the same, and her refusal is worrisome to Dad, who now appears to be leaning toward engaging her in physical contact, but is slipping more toward his "tortured, forehead-holding window-stumble" and, sure enough, he ends up gazing out the bay window, one knee lifted up to rest on the ledge, his head slumped into an open palm.

"I just don't get it, Joan. I can't do the dance, I can't talk the jargon. I thought it would be sitting at a desk and coming up with clever slogans or jingles, but it's not. It's like a tunnel of horror . . ."

"A tunnel of horror?"

"Whatever. A carnival haunted house. I have no idea what anyone's talking about. Everyone just seems to glide so effortlessly through all the crap, the meetings, the clients' whims. And the lunches, the dinners, the nights out, showing horrible people horrible bars with horrible thundering music and pretending to have fun. It's like the world was taken over before we were born by this supercynical race of practical jokers who decided to make everything as baffling and as fucked up as they could to see how much we could take. Only thing is, people are out there *flourishing* in this muck."

Dad turns from the window, blushing at what he has revealed. His eyes strain to meet Mom's.

"Look," Mom says, and Dad pales at the harshness in her voice. "All you need to do is to put the energy and determination you've put into your masterful lost-boy dance and its jargon into the sucking-up-to-the-client dance and *its* jargon." She stares him down and he turns back to the window. "One is not morally superior to the other." Mom spins back to her screen, which has been converted in her inattention to a cartoon of flying superheroes. She snaps them away with a touch of her mouse. "And the former is getting tiresome."

Dad is crushed. He picks up a glass paperweight and tosses it up and down, the rhythmic thud clashing with the antic pace of Mom's keystrokes. For a second, I picture him hurling the paperweight through the glass or at Mom's monitor or even at her head. My heart is pounding.

Quietly, he returns the paperweight to the pile of paper it was set upon and leaves the room, holding himself from slamming the door.

Immediately Mom stops keyboarding and stomps her feet like a small child throwing a tantrum. She pounds her fist onto the desk and runs to the door, which she throws open. She stands and looks up, toward the stairs Dad has ascended and she screams, "I am sick of being the only grown-up in this house!"

She steps back into her office and turns to look at me full in the face. She is red with anger. "And I am sick of pretending we don't see you always watching us! Stop *watching* us you little monster."

Dad and Mom make up later that night and after dinner they take a long walk. My sister and I clean up and afterward sit in the study listening to Glenn Miller. She is leafing through the latest edition of *Audubon* when she says, out of the blue, "No one knew how to tell you. It's probably best Mom did it like that, although you're probably mad at her now."

I cannot speak or even return her glance. The universe consists of one truth and no other: I am a buffoon.

"Look, spymaster, there's no such thing as objectivity, anyway. Your mission was doomed from the get-go."

I am a moron, an ape.

"Besides, the only thing you learn from watching people is how terror reduces their lives to tedium. And that's a story no one wants to hear."

Just then Mom and Dad walk in, giggling and wrapped in each other's arms. My sister rolls her eyes and then Dad announces that he is going to become a fireman, his childhood dream.

"I'm going to ride around in a big red truck!"

Jesus

I've been looking for a conversion experience. I've tried all the obvious places, the places you'd think you could find a conversion experience. I've sat on docks by the water at night, with the silver-lighted boats sliding by, I've stared at the immensity of the sky through an auburn-leafed oak from a bed of fallen leaves on a cool Massachusetts night. I've gone bowling, and, of course, I've gone to churches. I started out at the old historic churches—Trinity, Grace, St. Bart's. I'd sit in these places and look at the likenesses of Jesus in the stained glass and try to imagine the glory of his incarnation.

Mostly, though, what I do is try to picture Jesus walking through the desert in some crummy old pair of sandals, the son of God in a crummy pair of sandals. I listen for the sound of them trudging across the gravel. I listen for the sound of the parched desert air being drawn through his nostrils. He probably walked alone a lot. I read a book that suggested that the part of his life missing from the Bible—from when he was twelve until he was thirty—he spent in the East studying with Buddhists. This book suggested that a conspiracy of Church Fathers took that part out some time in the third century. I always liked the idea of Church Fathers; a bunch of guys in marble rooms with white beards—like a painting by David—studying ponderous texts in flowing robes, deciding maybe people didn't need to know about Jesus going to the East. I try not to think of things like that though when I'm looking for my conversion experience. I recognize such thoughts are distractions and I picture Jesus in the desert, a man alone in the desert with the sound of his own breath and the solitude of his thoughts.

There's a bowling alley a couple of blocks from work. Two or three times a week Jeannie and I go bowl a few games. She's about twenty years older than me, something she reminds me of frequently. I think she does that to remind us both that we aren't interested in each other romantically. She's a studio secretary and I'm the file clerk at a small industrial design firm. I didn't come to New York to be a file clerk but that is how it's worked out. The career world has turned out to be full of rules and maneuverings and a certain attitude that I both envy and despise. I watch the successful toss around their success, it floats around them like an aura and I can't for the life of me think how they sleep nights acting the way they do, so self-important, so ruthlessly determined, so meticulously groomed. I don't question their morality or ethics, just their stomachs: how do you act so foolishly and transparently and not hate yourself? And yet, can I honestly say I wouldn't sell my soul for a piece of it?

I usually get off work right at five but Jeannie almost always has to stay late. One of the associates will have a letter he needs typed or she'll have to do the FedEx labels. I wait for her in the pizza parlor across the street, eat a slice or two, take my time. I watch all the people pouring out of the buildings, getting taxis, heading for the trains. Then Jeannie will come bounding around the corner of our building, in her heels and a tight skirt, one of those long cigarettes hanging out of her mouth. She'll look both ways and cross University rolling her eyes, smiling and shaking her fists in the air. It's a joke with us that everyone we work for is an idiot.

Needless to say, nothing ever happens—no conversion experience anyway. And I do all the traditional stuff. I get down on my knees and pray and pray, "Please, Jesus, please, please come into my soul." I know it's crazy and it sounds southern and hillbilly-ish, but what can I say? My misery is tremendous. I hide it well though. People tell me I am the mellowest person they've ever met. That's a direct quote. A girl I used to work with said it. "You are the mellowest person I've ever met." Meanwhile, I feel like my eyes are about to melt, my ears gush blood, my heart pop right out of my chest. Meanwhile, I'm dying. "Please, Jesus, please," I say, picturing him in the desert, "please take my soul."

The other night I couldn't sleep. It was one of those horrible August heat wave nights. My fat old dog kept moving from the kitchen to the bathroom and panting and the Con Ed people were working all night right in front of my building. My futon, which I hate, seemed especially uncomfortable. I wanted to call somebody but it was after three in the morning. I wished I knew someone in California, where it was only midnight. For some reason the only person I could think of who lived in California was Johnny Carson. I wondered what he would be doing at midnight. I pictured him playing tennis—doubles with Bob Newhart, Don Rickles, and Steve Lawrence. Ed McMahon would be the line judge, sitting on the sidelines with a glass of scotch on ice. I'm sure Johnny Carson lives in a huge house; probably with a lighted tennis court.

I wanted to be crazy enough to call information in California and ask for his number, but I knew they wouldn't give it out. I thought, if I was that crazy it would make a funny story I could tell Jeannie in the morning and she'd laugh that crazy Jeannie laugh. "You won't believe what I did last night . . . ," I could say. But I'm not that crazy so I just got up and made an egg salad sandwich. I'd been going through a period where I was eating almost nothing but egg salad sandwiches. I'll do that for weeks at a time. Eat the same thing all day long whenever I get hungry no matter if it's a mealtime or not. I'll whip up a big bowl of egg salad or tuna salad or whatever and just eat sandwich after sandwich, biting off big mouthfuls, one right after the next, bored half out of my mind.

I got back from the kitchen with my sandwich and flipped through the channels and, incredibly, I found the movie *Jesus Christ Superstar*. I knew what it was right away. It was a scene where Jesus and all the disciples drive a school bus out into the desert somewhere, some empty piece of nowhere, and they all jump out, all these hippies, like this is the greatest place they've ever seen, like orphans at Disneyworld, and they sing and sing.

They say there are two kinds of people. Those who are willing to accept the suspension of reality in musicals and listen to people sing to each other in circumstances that don't really call for song. (As if there are *any* circumstances that do.) And then there are those, like me, who just hate it every time someone breaks into song. I always think, I'm sure they just *sing*. The point of all this is that I thought it was a sign, that maybe there'd be a message for me in *Jesus Christ Superstar*, but I couldn't stand all the singing. Not to mention a bus, a yellow American school bus in the ancient Near East.

As a kid I would watch the evangelists on TV. That's when it started, the throbbing and the panic, and for some reason I thought of Jesus as being the one to go to. I remember the day my brother came home for his first weekend back from college. I was thirteen and I was sitting up in my room listening to him talk and laugh with my parents around the kitchen table and my head was spinning because I had no idea how to walk down the stairs and say hello to my brother. I couldn't imagine how such a thing was done. Maybe because I'd never seen such a scene acted out on TV. Eventually I went down, stumbling and blushing, extending an awkward hand to the silent room, which, for some reason caused stifled laughs that made my eyes feel like lead.

I started praying with the evangelists then at night, after everyone had gone to bed, my hands touching the image of theirs on the screen. "Please, Jesus, please."

I'm just a guy who wants a little relief, who wants the throbbing to stop. I don't want to save the world, or make your kids pray in school, or outlaw abortion. I don't want to wear polyester, go to Heritage USA, or carry the Bible in my back pocket. I just want to be able to walk out the door in the morning without feeling like my eyes are going to burst. I just want the fears to go away and to be able to look people in the eye as I pass them on the street. I want the echo chamber in my head to soften its thunder.

Jeannie doesn't know about any of this. Nobody does. I figure you just work this stuff out on your own. Meanwhile, you take care of the other stuff the best you can. Go to work, do your laundry, bowl with Jeannie. Jeannie is a moody, very unpredictable woman. She goes with a guy out in New Jersey. He's a construction worker named Tony and she talks about him all the time. He doesn't treat her very well. He's never had her out to his house and Jeannie is starting to think maybe he's married. Sometimes he doesn't call her for a week—sometimes longer. She tells me this stuff and I don't really know what to say. "Some guys are like that," I tell her and she looks up at me, her eyes squinting in the smoke from her cigarette. "Bowl," she says in spectacular Jeannie deadpan, "just bowl."

Which I do. I truly enjoy bowling. I love the sounds of a bowling alley. All that rumbling, the reset machine, the ball returns. And all the sounds just bounce around forever inside those big cavernous rooms. All the people around you are having a good time. People are happy when they're bowling, even though most of them aren't very good at all. It's like golf; a few show-offs and then there's everybody else. People drink beer, the women act loose. It's nice. Being in a bowling alley is a feeling I wish I could carry with me when I leave.

The bowling alley we go to is on the fourth floor. You have to take an elevator to get there. It's a tiny little elevator that moves very slowly and needs to be operated manually. Sometimes there's a line of people spilling out into the street waiting to be taken up to the bowling alley. The guy who runs the elevator is notoriously unfriendly. He scowls at you and tells you you only have to ring the bell *once*.

When I was back in Ohio recently to visit my family I tried a few of those Danish modern churches—those suburban churches that sprang up all over the place in the sixties. I thought maybe if the old city churches didn't do it, maybe these would. Of course, I didn't tell my family what I was doing. Usually I just told them I was going to the mall and I would make some joke about how there are no malls in Manhattan, how I missed the recirculated air, the fluorescent lights and the terra-cotta planters.

One night after bowling Jeannie needed to talk. She never said that to me before; usually she just talks. She seemed serious. She was distracted all through our games and she bowled horribly. "Okay," I said as we waited for the unfriendly man to take us back to the street. Jeannie suggested we go to the coffee shop across the street and talk. It was the second time she used the word "talk" and that made me nervous. I thought it was Tony. Maybe he hit her. That would be the next logical step in their relationship, he'd start hitting her.

The coffee shop was freezing cold, only nobody else seemed to notice. I shivered the moment Jeannie pulled open the door. The air was so thick and cold I imagined I could see it, a frigid white blast rolling over itself onto University Place. I looked around at everyone. They all seemed fine—eating their cheeseburgers, their roast chickens, their Greek salads, clanking their thick white cups with little pools of coffee in their saucers. I always get an eerie feeling walking into a restaurant, especially coffee shops in the city, with everyone packed in so tightly and the lights so bright. They're all having their own conversations. It's not like the collective noise of a bowling alley, which feels dispersed and safe, almost hypnotic.

Jeannie smoked one cigarette after another. When I looked at her questioningly she blew out some smoke and said we'd eat first and talk after. I could see this was very hard for her, which was odd. Usually she just blurts stuff out between frames. Intimate stuff. Stuff you'd think I had no business knowing.

Jeannie and I had been friends for a couple of months. She's new at the office. Most everyone else there seems at a loss as to what to make of me. The graphics woman used to talk to me while I filed. She'd come and smoke cigarettes and ask me questions about what I thought about New York living. She was full of stories about outrageous real estate scams involving thousand-dollar finder fees for tiny studios in bad neighborhoods and just kept saying, "It is *such* a scam!" Eventually she gave up on me though. I think it was right about the time she asked me what I was "really, you know, an actor or something." I think she thought my answer that I'm just a guy who does the filing was cocky. People often think of me as cocky or sarcastic or arrogant. I just never know what they want. What do people want? And what is so weird about being the file guy? What is there to *explain* in that?

A few nights after I wanted to call Johnny Carson but watched *Jesus Christ Superstar* instead, I had a dream. In it, I was Jesus, walking alone through the immense silence of the desert. All I could hear was the sound of the little rocks under my sandals, my breathing, and the wind. I was breathing very heavily. I had been walking a very long time and knew I still had a tremendous distance yet to go. I was on my way to the East to study with the Buddhists. I'd known I was the son of God for a long time now. It came to me one night, just like that: "You are the son of God." So

I set off for the East to study with the Buddhists. I was thinking about what a far journey it was from Nazareth to the East, especially for a twelve year old on his own for the first time. I was wondering why there weren't any Buddhists that lived closer I could study with. Or, why I hadn't just been born in the East. That way I could study with the Buddhists and then head over to the Mediterranean to do all the rest. Then I'd only have to make the journey once, instead of having to go all the way out there and then come all the way back. But what really made the journey hard was that, as the son of God, I was omniscient, and being omniscient I knew that a few centuries down the road there'd be a conspiracy of Church Fathers and they would destroy all records of my journey from Nazareth to the East to study with the Buddhists. But I had to go ahead and make it anyway. That's what really sucked: having the knowledge, but having to make the journey anyway.

Jeannie finally got around to talking to me after she finished her dinner. She had the flounder au gratin with potatoes and a salad with creamy Italian on the side. The salad was a big chunk of iceberg lettuce and a slice of tomato in a plastic bowl made to look like it was wood. She got a little bowl of broccoli too but she didn't want that so it just sat there through most of her dinner until finally I just ate it. "Well," she said after the olive-skinned waitress had removed all the empty plates, "I suppose you're wondering what this is all about." She sounded like an Agatha Christie novel. I nodded. "I don't want you to take this the wrong way. I really care about you and I've enjoyed the time we've spent together, but, uhm, well let me just put it this way. I'm worried about you. You're young. You're just a kid. You're good looking, smart, funny. You live in Manhattan, the most exciting city in the world, and what do you do with yourself? You bowl with a middle-aged secretary." She was by now looking terribly uncomfortable, growing nearly pale. "I mean, you live hundreds of miles from your family, you don't seem to have any other friends." She looked down at her ashtray, cleared her throat. "Do you . . . have any other friends?"

I looked away, over her shoulder, my head pounding.

"You could be living this life in Iowa."

"Ohio!" I corrected her. "Why is that so hard to remember?" I asked, nearly shouting. She was one of these people, New Yorkers mostly, who just think it's all the same out there. When people find out I'm from Ohio they ask me about cows and cornfields. In fifteen years in Ohio the closest I ever got to a cow or a cornfield was whizzing past them on the interstate.

"Whatever," she said, "Iowa, Ohio, whatever the hell it is. There're middle-aged secretaries out there you could be bowling with." I fidgeted in my seat. "Listen, don't get upset. I'm just worried you're unhappy, that you're alone and unhappy."

I had nothing to say. I never do, really. When you get right down to the core, if you hold a mirror up to me you find there's nothing there. If you pull away the rules I'm a statue, cold and unmoving. There's nothing there and I know it. It's no surprise to me. I've been having this conversation all my life. Teachers, roommates at school, my mother and father. "What's wrong?" they ask, after getting me alone. It's like the Inquisition. Does everyone suffer through these confrontations? I can't imagine that they do.

Jeannie finally just left. She said she was starting to feel pressure to be my mother, "or something." She paid the bill and just slipped out of the booth. "Sorry," she said, as I cringed, thinking everyone was listening and had been throughout. I hated her. Her face was huge and ugly and full of wrinkles and blemishes. I'd never noticed before how many wrinkles she had. And the fat that hung from below her chin had veins running through it. She was hideous.

A few days later, I was sitting in Grace Church staring through the stained glass. The maintenance person of the church, an Arabic-looking man not much older than myself who I saw in there all the time, was changing lightbulbs in the tiny chandeliers suspended from the vaulted ceiling, probably two stories above the floor. He had a wooden ladder, one of the kind that suspends itself, forming a triangle with the floor, and he moved it with great effort from chandelier to chandelier, each time climbing it with a look of stark terror on his face. I couldn't understand why he was doing this plainly dangerous job alone. I was going to get up and at least hold the bottom steady for him, but just as I was about to a group of Italian tourists came in, chatting and laughing. The brightness of their clothes and the confidence in their European swagger intimidated me, and I got up and left. The sun was blinding as I stumbled down the steps onto the street.

In my dream I eventually became aware that I was dreaming I was Jesus. I knew I was lying on my little uncomfortable futon on 48th Street dreaming I was Jesus and started trying to direct things. I started thinking: this is it, this has got to be it. I'm dreaming I'm Jesus on my way to the East to study with the Buddhists. I've got two major religions here. There'll have to be something here for me. I struggled to have my conversion experience. But the more I struggled, the closer I got to waking up. I panicked then and tried to pretend I wasn't waiting for my conversion experience. I tried to go back, but, of course, that doesn't work.

More and more, I think the only way I'm going to get my conversion experience is to stop waiting for it, which to me seems impossible. It's like when I lie awake in bed at night with the sound of my dog's breathing keeping me awake. I try and try not to listen to it, but the more I try, the louder and more irritating it gets until it seems like it's the only sound in the world. Eventually, of course, I do forget the sound and I fall asleep. That's the moment I need. The moment I stop hearing the noise. But, of course, that's the moment I can never remember. Ever. No matter how hard I try.

I put in my notice at work the day after Jeannie and I had dinner. I figured I can file anywhere. On my last day I left early because I saw someone sneaking a cake box and a bag of two-liter bottles of soft drinks into the office. I rode the train home with my head pounding.

The Main Event

Right around the Fourth my Uncle Len, who had just moved in with us, started having his murder dream. Then my girlfriend, Lola, told me she was pregnant—and to add misery to confusion, the air conditioning went out just as it started getting really hot. We'd just gotten a new heat pump after years and years of my father refusing even to consider something so extravagant as central air. When it broke down he got all huffy about how he told us so and he gave us his "People Have Been Getting Along Just Fine for Centuries Without . . ." speech and we all just supposed we should just let it go.

Uncle Len is my mother's brother and he came to live with us when his third wife committed suicide, just like his first had. His second ran away with another man to Indiana. My mother said he was thinking there was something wrong with him so she asked him to come live with us for a while. She told us she wanted him to see what a real family was like. She thought his wives had all been trashy women. I didn't know the first one. She hung herself in the backyard from a tree when I was in kindergarten. The second one, Irene, used to come over without him late at night with a bottle of wine and shout at my mother about what a skunk her brother was. Then there was Josie who waitressed and wouldn't give it up after the wedding because she said she met such interesting people. They came over a lot. Josie mostly popped her gum and fiddled with her brastraps. She killed herself by tying a plastic bag around her neck in the bathtub after drinking half a magnum of Mad Dog. My Uncle Len found both his dead wives and caught Irene in bed with her boyfriend. My father told me all those things, the details. He said Len was a clod and told me that a man who marries floozies deserves what he gets. "A wife isn't for fun," he told me. "We aren't here to have fun."

In Uncle Len's murder dream he wakes up from sleeping (in the dream) and thinks he's just woken up from a bad dream. Then he goes and gets a butcher knife from the kitchen and kills us all, one at a time. He carves us up "like turkeys, starting with James." I heard him one night telling my parents this; he was sweating with fear after waking up screaming. I was listening from the upstairs banister.

It chilled me that he started his massacre with me, and I wondered what Freud would think of his dream. In the spring we'd studied Freud in psychology class and ever since I'd been fascinated by dreams and the subconscious mind, two worlds where everything and anything can happen, but where nothing exists. I met Lola in that class. We used to sit in the back row and roll our eyes at how stupid everyone seemed. She was the first person I ever met who understood, who saw the world like I did. We both loved Freud and knew instinctively that he was a genius. Our first dates were spent sitting in the parking lot behind the old Laundromat tossing stones at garbage cans and talking about the invisible world of the mind, how it silently ruled the lives of man.

She was brilliant, I thought, and talked passionately. Then we started having sex, which she did with equal passion. And now, just this week, she told me she thinks she's pregnant.

My mother is a firm believer in chores and one of mine is to feed the chinchillas that live in the basement. My mother was raising chinchillas to sell for their fur in tiny chicken wire cages all over the basement. They were loud and obnoxious and smelled awful, but she thought someday they would put us on Easy Street. Which, she said, was "farther than your father will ever get us." She thought my father didn't work hard enough and didn't exert himself. They argued about it all the time. "You've got to put yourself out there," she'd say, holding open a paperback "How To" book at her hip as proof that she knew what she was talking about. She was always reading books about succeeding in the business world. My father never read them and this was a source of a lot of fights. "How can you just turn your back on Easy Street?" she would cry. "What kind of a man are you?" Things like that. If nothing else, these fights proved what my father said, you don't get married for fun.

My mother told me not to get too attached to the chinchillas because soon they would be goners, but there was no problem there. I hated those damn animals with their buckteeth and smelly racks of pellets. I wouldn't have cared if the house caught on fire and they burned alive.

The day Lola told me she thought she was pregnant, I went down there like always and fed the damn things out of the big feed bags my mother bought and I noticed one of them was having babies. Not an uncommon event, but still, like a lot of things, it made me mad at God. There's a lot I don't understand, even with Claude the Genius' whisperings, and I've decided that the reason I don't understand them is that God doesn't want me to. The world could have been created to be understood, but it wasn't. And *that,* it seems to me, is pure maliciousness—on God's part. Take for instance the dinosaurs, or why the universe is so big and Earth such a tiny speck of nothingness. You would think that there is some kind of a reason for everything, and if there is, why were there dinosaurs on Earth so long before men? What were they doing here? Why didn't Creation just start with us? Were the dinosaurs just a practice run for the main event, or is there some reason behind their multimillion-year reign? Claude the Genius tells me in my sleep that they were here because they were an important part of the food chain that today has turned into oil and coal and God wanted us to have oil and coal so we could drive Toyotas and have stereos. But if that's true, then it's possible that *we* aren't even the main event. Maybe the point is for us to destroy ourselves so the real reason the universe was created can get started. Maybe God is up there twiddling his thumbs and yawning. Meanwhile, we think he's watching all the sparrows fall.

So I watched the chinchilla squirting out another half-dozen or so smelly fur coats and I looked up at God, although all I saw was heating ducts, and said, in as sarcastic a voice as possible, "Oh, I suppose there's a message here for me, eh?" I thought this because, obviously, I had abortions on my mind. Lola would have to get one. I was not going to be a father at fifteen. And that was that. Period. Thank you very much. So then I get a nature film in living color about the glory of reproduction. Ha-ha, God, good one.

At dinner that night Uncle Len said he thought maybe he would check himself into a loony bin. My mother said that nobody was checking into any loony bin because nobody was loony. Then Uncle Len said, "I'd just hate to wake up one morning and find you all dead and cut up."

"So would we, Len," my father cheered, his mouth full of creamed broccoli, "so would we."

He was trying to be funny, which I thought was really his only option, but my mother just glared at him.

"One of the chinchillas had six babies today," I announced, my voice echoing in my own head in a strange way, like it wasn't even me talking.

"Hello, Easy Street!" my mother said, her fork raised high in victory.

The next day I went into town to see Lola at her job. She worked in the ladies apparel section of her grandfather's old department store. Lola's grandfather, Herb Dickens, was one of the richest men in town. Dickens' department store had been at the heart of the old downtown for almost a hundred years. But now a new mall was going up and everyone said he would go out of business. Lola didn't care. She said she had her trust fund and was going to move to L.A. and become a movie star like Meryl Streep—not for the money or the fame, she told me, but because fantasy is all she'd ever known or been comfortable with. "And," she said, "I'll have an edge over all the other girls, because I won't have to waitress or fuck anybody for money. I've got a trust fund."

I stood over by the cash register while Lola finished up with a customer. The woman was trying on flannel blazers but couldn't decide which one best showed off her eyes. Lola seemed impatient and then the woman finally just decided on the blue-green plaid and paid with cash. "People," Lola told me as she whisked me down the steps, "are just absolutely stupid and that's all there is to it."

We had lunch in the town square, which was swimming in flags and banners for the Fourth. They'd even dragged out the old fire truck and there were two shirtless men with crew cuts washing it about fifty yards from where we sat with our sandwiches from Sally's. A firehouse dog watched the firemen from the shade of the gazebo. Occasionally the men would squirt each other and curse.

"*Of course* I'm getting an abortion," Lola said after I made my "We're Too Young to Have Children" speech—which I'd been practicing all morning. "Don't be stupid. The thing is *how*? I can't get at my trust fund until I'm eighteen." While we sat there, supposedly trying to think about how we would pay for the abortion, I was really thinking about Lola and her trust fund. I tried to imagine how the world must seem to someone who knew that after she turned eighteen she would never in her life worry about money.

Finally I asked how much an abortion costs and then we both just looked at each other. She said she would try and find out and then we walked back to Dickens'. On the way we passed my

Uncle Len and he told me to come by and see him after dropping Lola off. I kissed her under Dickens' ancient awning, right in front of some customers, and she whispered in my ear, "While I'm pregnant we won't have to use a rubber." And she squeezed my thigh. That was the odd thing about her being pregnant; even though we both hated them, we always used rubbers—which are 99 percent effective, or so they taught us in health class.

Uncle Len wasn't working, and rather than spend his days getting out of the way of my mother's vacuuming, he drank coffee at the Starlight Diner and read the paper. I saw him in there a lot and usually pretended I hadn't. But that day I went in and joined him at his booth. "Hi'ya kiddo," he said uneasily. He hadn't shaved and I thought he looked like the kind of guy you see on the news being arrested for stabbing a family to death for no reason. "That girl of yours is something." He whistled to show me how much he thought of her. "Kids today are so lucky. The only way I'll ever get in the pants of a fifteen year old is to get a Bangkok whore. Enjoy it," he grinned, "life does nothing but get weirder."

Janice the waitress came by and I told her I wanted a cup of coffee.

There was a chance Uncle Len was going insane, but I thought he'd led an interesting life and was probably the type of guy that knew about things like abortions. So as I sipped my coffee I told him the whole story and asked his advice. He smoked with squinted eyes as I finished and then he leaned forward and told me this was the oldest trick in the book. He said Lola was trapping me into marrying her. He said he knew this because no woman would say what she said to me about not using a rubber. "A pregnant woman is not like a regular woman," he said. "Their brains go to mush and they don't think about sex like that. They've already got some damn thing growing down there and they don't want men showering it with their stuff." He said she wanted to have sex with me without a rubber so she would *get* pregnant and then she would make me marry her so I'd have to support her for the rest of her life.

"But she has a trust fund, Uncle Len," I told him. "She's already got more money than I'll ever have."

"Oh yeah," he said. "I forgot she was a Dickens."

We sat there for a while in silence and I felt kind of sorry for him. He'd been so excited when he was warning me about Lola's conspiracy, and now I'd robbed him of that. "Damn!" he said finally. "That body *and* a trust fund. *You* should pretend to get pregnant."

When I got home my mother was reading Lee Iacocca's autobiography on the screened-in porch. She was dressed in striped shorts and a blouse. The tails of her blouse she had tied in knots so that her belly button showed. "This world," she said to me, dropping the book in her lap, "is like a chastity belt. All that exists between you and paradise is a key. That's all you need: the key. And then it's all yours. Do you know how rich Lee Iacocca is?"

I didn't know.

"He's rich," she said, nodding her head, "let's just say that: he's rich. And do you know what it is that he knows that your father doesn't?"

It wasn't my day. I didn't know that either.

"That *it's possible*. Think about that James. That's the only thing you need to know." She stared at me for a while and I tried not to look at one of her nipples that was showing. But then she followed my eyes down her throat and pulled her blouse closed. "Oh, yeah, Lola called. She said you're on for tonight."

I didn't know what that meant since we hadn't made any plans. Except, of course, for rubberless sex, in honor of her pregnancy. So if that's what she meant, I was all for it. It was time to feed the chinchillas, though, so I went downstairs and dragged out the big dusty bag of feed and made the rounds. The newborns were still squiggly pink blobs the size of my thumb and were all thrown together in a pile behind their mother. I thought of their journey in life, living out the eternity of it here in our basement and then being butchered so we could get some money for their fur. They would never once see the sun or the grass or any of that stuff people write poems about. Claude the Genius told me one night, in his steely nocturnal whispers, that if I was ever going to truly learn anything it would be from the plight of "those poor creatures in your basement." He told me I should consider our mastery over their fate without their compliance or understanding as comparable to the mystery of creation. The only problem was that I hated the things—so messy and loud and smelly. But I decided maybe I would try and feel compassion for them and started by naming the newborns. I named one Claude, one Freud, one Lola, and then one for each of Uncle Len's wives, the two suicides and the runaway.

Two days later it was the Fourth and I went with Lola to a barbecue at her grandfather's mansion, Stillwater Estate. It was a huge old house up on a hill that overlooked the old riverbed where the Army Corps of Engineers was building something no one was supposed to know anything about, although everyone had a theory. There were lots of people at the party and my mother would've killed to be one of them, but Lola said it wasn't for her to invite anyone since it wasn't her party. There was a senator there.

Lola had found out how to get an abortion and we had one scheduled for two weeks away. She said it was too much fun having sex without a rubber to rush into anything that could just as well wait. "Besides, I don't have morning sickness or anything." She said being pregnant didn't feel at all different than not being pregnant. "None of that magic mother stuff women on TV always get so goo-goo about." I was worried about waiting two weeks but didn't say anything because I knew it was her decision. Also, I loved having sex without a rubber—except it usually ended much faster. She was getting an advance on her salary to pay for it and said I could contribute half if I ever got a job but I shouldn't worry about it because she had a trust fund.

After dinner Lola took me on a tour of the house, which seemed to be falling apart. The stairways all creaked and a couple of banisters were loose. The downstairs was really the only part of the house that got cleaned regularly because that is where Mr. Dickens spent all his time. He'd moved his bedroom to the old library when the stairs got to be too much for him. The decorations were very elegant and I felt like I was in a museum more than like I was in a house. In one room there was a huge harpsichord with a bust of Napoleon sitting on top of it. Lola sat down at the keyboard and played the opening of "Stairway to Heaven" and when she got to the part where it was time to sing I started, "There's a lady who's sure, all that glitters is gold, and she's buying the stairway to hea-eave-en," I sang and then we both started laughing.

On the second floor there were a lot of old bedrooms with furniture that was all dusty and unused. She showed me the room she used to stay in when she visited as a child. It had a giant canopy bed that was covered with scary old dolls with porcelain heads and glass eyes. In the corner was a huge wardrobe that Lola said she used to sit in while she masturbated. "I was so afraid of getting caught." She said it got so hot in there one time from her breathing that she momentarily passed out and she would've suffocated to death, she said, if she hadn't fallen into the door, pushing it open. "So I woke up half in and half out of this wardrobe with nothing on and it was so scary because I had no idea who I was or where I was." She said that's how it is when you pass out: you wake up and you could be anyone, anywhere, with any past. "But then it all comes back to you. For better or worse."

The third floor was the dustiest, darkest, and scariest. There was even an old mannequin, a headless one wearing a yellowed bodice. In the corner was a round window that looked out at the lawn where the picnickers were. Lola looked out of it and then called me over. She pushed it open and we stared down at everyone. "Did you ever feel like you could do anything, like you really can't rule anything out? Like maybe someday you'd kill someone just to see what that felt like?"

I said I did most things I did just to see how it would feel, but that I didn't think I could kill anyone.

"Never say never," she said letting us fall into a silence. I noticed her eyes growing wide. A slight breeze rustled her hair. She held my hand then and brought it to her mouth, kissing it gently. "My man," she said, practically whispering. Then she turned back to the window. "Like the senator," she said, pointing down into the crowd. "There's a rifle up here. I know where it is and I know that it's loaded. We could shoot him. I wouldn't feel a thing. I could just watch him drop; and then the screaming and I could just walk away. We could have sex. I'd never think of it again. That's why I'm going to be such a good actress. I've always been acting, it's just now I'm going to find people to pay me for it."

We didn't shoot the senator, but we did have rubberless sex in her old bed surrounded by all her old dolls. Afterward, when we were lying in bed I played with the dolls. I noticed that if you held them upside down their eyelids closed with a little whispering click. As I held one, I decided to tell Lola about Claude the Genius and his nighttime visits to me. I'd never mentioned him to anyone before, but I thought since she told me she would maybe like to kill someone, I owed her a secret. Claude the Genius was the only one I had. I told her the story of how a voice whispers to me in my sleep, how he told me his name was Claude and that he was a genius from another dimension that couldn't be described in any way that would mean anything to me, and how he tries to explain the mysteries of the universe. "But even with his help, I still don't get it," I told her. She held me tight and stared into my eyes with wonder.

"You are chosen," she said, "*chosen.*" And then she climbed on top of me and we rubbed our sweat-soaked bodies together, staring into each other's eyes in absolute silence.

Then it started to get dark out and it was time to go see the fireworks. Mr. Dickens paid for them every year so he got a big section of seats right in front of the grandstands they built in the town square. We all drove downtown in a caravan of Cadillacs. Lola and me actually rode with Mr. Dickens; an honor. He smoked cigars and talked about how the world was going to hell. He said that Maoists were massing at the borders, just waiting for the opportunity to pour across, a tidal wave of revolutionaries, collectivizing everything. "You'll see," he said. "They're coming. One day you'll be pricing tampons at the strip mall, and the next you'll be herding chickens at a reeducation camp in Arkansas."

In town we walked right past my mother and father and Uncle Len. They had terrible seats way back in the vacant lot across from the square. I pretended not to see them even though I could feel my mother's eyes. Soon after we arrived Mr. Dickens nodded to a man who lit a flashlight to tell the detonators to begin. Lola held tightly onto my arm and breathed hard into my neck. "Isn't it all just so absolutely thrilling," she said, the sky ablaze and our seats vibrating with the explosions. "We've tamed chaos and taught it to dance." A series of white-hot M-100s exploded in quick succession like something trying to bust through the sky, like we were on the inside of a drum being pounded. Lola said again that "anything is possible," and though the idea thrilled her, it scared me. Claude the Genius called it the "Dictatorship of Chance" and said we were destined to live under its rule without relief or redress until the circle of time collapsed upon itself.

The finale was spectacular. A full five and a half minutes worth of explosions and light. It left everyone breathless and desperate for more, but ultimately resigned to the fact that it would be another year's wait.

The Last of the Plaids

"If you count to ten, before you get to seven, you'll see a jerk." This is what Marcy says as she twists her wrist to right her watch, which she wears loose like a bracelet and whose face has spun to the inside of her wrist, the side you slice when committing suicide. She has just had her hair cut—for the first time in the many years I have been among the fold (worshiping her). It is a drastic cut—from below the shoulders to above the ears—but Marcy has taken it in stride, amazing us all. She has retained her composure so well, in fact, you can hardly notice her hair's been cut at all. Except that nine inches of it is gone, of course. It is astonishing, but it is believable, in a very Marcyesque way, that she has already grown into her new look.

She runs her long, delicate fingers across her scalp seemingly at ease.

Some of us exchange looks at Marcy's proclamation. She is rarely so ungenerous toward her fellow man, rarely so cynical. "Think about it," she says, turning from face to enraptured face, "this world is *swimming* in jerks." She has a point certainly. Most of us nod in assent. Some more easily than others. I guess there are about nine of us these days, although it is hard to say exactly with some people in the tentative throes of joining and some in the equally tentative throes of leaving. We are arranged around her in a crescent, seated at a banquet table covered in a cloth of slightly stained linen.

Perhaps there are others—I am sure of it in fact—who, if taken aside, would characterize the nature of their relationship to Marcy as one of worshiper/worshipee. Although maybe they would not be as free in admitting this as I am. Who can say for sure? Marcy, perhaps. I suppose she knows a good deal more about the others than I like to think. I know she knows of my worship. I've whispered the secret of it into her soft, downy ears more than once, more than twice, even. She's *seemed* moved, as though my confession meant to her in the hearing of it as much as it did to me in the speaking of it. I suppose it's possible though, that Marcy hears such confessions routinely. Perhaps they are but an amusing, predictable but essentially meaningless sidelight to her life. Maybe they would be fifteenth on her list of occurrences on a given day. "Oh, yes, I nearly forgot," she might say while unpacking groceries, "X told me again that he worships me. Oh, damn, I forgot the corn!" We know so little. It's amazing *any*thing ever happens between people.

Tonight one of the others will pay. One of the young ones. They have been looking to me as an elder of late, as though age alone has endowed me with fortune. The fools! And these checks are getting big. And not just from the expansion of the fold. I think some of the others are hoarding food, stuffing their pockets with crab puff appetizers and club sandwich quarters. Guzzling drinks. Aside from that, I've noticed some queer behavior. Snide remarks. And more than once I could've sworn I felt the slight breeze caused by a madly swung leg. Have we resorted to kicking each other?!

Things are changing. The times. There was a day when a sense of harmony existed among us all. Now the air is thick with competition, so thick at times it is hard to catch your breath. It wasn't that in the old days we were all so keen on sharing, but there was an understanding that what we all craved, and received, was as much a product of our communal craving as it was what Marcy herself was giving. The whole created the parts and the parts created the whole, and with this we were happy. Who wouldn't be?

But something has happened even to Marcy. She is usually quite cheery. I notice her eyeing Y, who, by the way, has been grooming himself in a way I can only describe as pandering. I discussed it one recent evening with Z as we walked home, huddling close by each other's side for protection in these increasingly violent streets. Z suspects tailoring, but I happen to know, approximately, Y's income and it prohibits *that* level of extravagance. I suspect he has simply found a good wholesaler. My concern was the mousse and the scrupulously maintained three-day's growth of stubble. It is my belief that there should be a level playing field. Z agrees but suggests I may be hopelessly naive in today's world.

Marcy is definitely eyeing Y, flashing double takes in his direction, smiling coyly. I glance at Z and see that he shares my concern. I am definitely not picking up the check! Let Y pay! Him and his mousse and his Italian slacks!

Marcy has now become metaphysical. Strangely, suddenly, with just a cock of her head she asks if, when looking into a mirror, it is the reflection we perceive or the reflection's perception of the physical body standing before the mirror. "Do we look at ourselves with the eyes of the reflection, or do we look at the reflection?" None of us know how to respond. A siren wails by in the street and Marcy glares at the maître d' who scurries to pull even tighter the heavy leaden doors with the thick red drapes. Even Y, lately so graceful and at ease in his pandering outfit, struggles to assume the correct posture to: (a) appease Marcy this interruption (one of her areas of grave intolerance); and (b) answer correctly her unanswerable question. I watch as he squirms while the maître d' bows over to Marcy and whispers ingratiatingly into her ear. My heart sinks. I stare at the distance between his moving lips and Marcy's soft ear and I ache. The maître d' bows and leaves, walking backwards, blowing kisses. And Marcy smiles. "Now," she says, "what was I saying?" She looks to me as the elder of the group and I lie. I don't know how or why I just do, and as I do I watch the relief spread across my fellows' worried faces. Furrowed brows flatten and ties are loosened—slightly. "Rats," I say, "you were asking us about rats." It is a plausible lie and this is what contributes to the general easing of tensions. Rats are one of Marcy's favorite subjects and we are always encouraged to share new rat stories whenever we have one. Marcy shudders in a girlish way and her eyes widen. One of the new fellows begins a story. I see he is nervous, speaking up for the first time in the group. And his story is good. About a friend who woke in the night with a rat nibbling on his toes. It is familiar, but he tells it with gusto not knowing we have heard many similar, so it succeeds and Marcy squeals in delight. Y then tells a story of garbage men chasing one across the Avenue late one night and hitting it back and forth with tire irons like a sport. And the crowd of late-night wanderers that gathered to cheer them on. "It was a community feeling you don't much get anymore," Y says, drifting into an affected melancholia.

If seniority counted for anything, I would have it made. I knew Marcy when she was a kid, long before all the commotion, back when she had trouble even getting a date. Don't scoff! Such a day truly existed. (This is the problem with the young, they can't imagine things having existed prior to their experiencing them, that things went along just fine even before they were there to watch.) I know it's hard to believe, to look at her now, radiant with light and wisdom and magnetism. Once I held her as she wept from loneliness. Don't laugh! It's true. Marcy wept onto my very own shoulder. Staining, as a matter of fact, a blazer of mine, the last of the plaids I used to own so many of, before solids came back. It hangs still in my closet.

But seniority doesn't matter in this world where we spend our days performing mindless tasks in cluttered offices and noisy shops, our nights plodding our way through the devastation, scurrying from haven to haven. The deep, sighing release of sanctuary has become our only joy. Everything is shrinking, most noticeably our expectations. What used to be a mere by-product of happiness has itself *become* happiness. The rungs of the ladder are fewer and fewer, the rhapsody of escape plays quieter and on simpler scales. The ascent is now fueled by fear of what seethes below rather than anticipation of what chimes above. And through it all we forget what came before because not to would leave us deadened—more so even than we are. History is our enemy. Contrary to the popular axioms, it teaches us nothing but what is gone, providing a yardstick no one wants to confront. And yet as the elder, history is what I possess the most of, an obsolete weapon. My memories of Marcy in a historyless world are useless to me—an absurdity, like the grasslands' targetless missile silos.

Maybe it's been too long. (How do you know when it's been too long?) Others have come and gone. More, in fact, than I would care to mention. There was a time when I felt self-conscious about them. I'd watch the glow they came into the fold with—that wide-eyed wonderment—fade into, what is it? Disillusion? Boredom? I used to fear it would get me too, that one day the spell would fade and I too would drift. I'd lie awake nights fearing the shatter and fighting to subdue the butterflies in my stomach at the thought of being set adrift. I would struggle to remember: how had I filled my days before Marcy? What were my nights like? Around whose image were my dreams constructed? But the answer lay in days so distant, in years and my ability to recall them, that they had, practically speaking, ceased even to exist. Before Marcy, the truth is, I *was not*.

Self-awareness breeds self-doubt. We all know that. Self-awareness actually is self-doubt. That's the conclusion I finally drew on those tortured nights. To shut, as well as I could, these relentlessly inward-probing eyes and simply allow myself the pleasure of the fold, to simply bask in Marcy's presence, letting the grandeur of it wash over me. This would have to be enough. If it is all that was being given, it would simply have to be enough. But now it looks like such consolations were foolhardy, the interior whisperings and rationalizations of a failure dressing his failings in less soul-deadening attire, creating a reality in words that explain the absence of deeds in a way that keeps nooses untied, razors in shavers, and barrels of guns away from temples.

Y, I see through tearing eyes, is definitely moving in for the kill. We have exhausted all the new rat stories and he has moved closer and is relating a series of vaguely sexual anecdotes, one right after another, that Marcy listens to, raptly, even at times with a wicked grin. During his tale of the stir caused at his office by a secretary who one day wore only a bodysuit to work, Marcy slowly extended her slender fingers, like a prowling spider, across the table and actually touched him. The contact, you could see, sent a shiver through him, and, in turn, through the rest of us. But Y kept his cool, smiling and continuing his story, describing the musculature of her thighs as highlighted by her bodysuit. "And what were the men saying?" Marcy asked. "Tell me their comments." And he did! The brazenness! It left us all speechless.

Maybe it was inevitable that one among us would trespass the rules. As I sit here watching him wade in waters none of us were ever before brave enough to endure, it seems the only sensible course, the only logical action. And I would have done it myself if only it had occurred to me or if I would have had the strength or the vision or the luck or the imagination for it. I look among us and sense I am not alone in my envy and self-flagellation. I see a sea of deflated faces as we watch Marcy wiggle in her seat and listen to her shower purrs and moans on another—for all but Y, it is on another.

The night ends and eyes dance and avert and Marcy stands to thank us all again for a wonderful, wonderful evening. She tells us again how much it all has meant to her, how highly she regards all our affection and then she paces the crescent of us, stopping to kiss delicately each proffered cheek. She loiters revealingly at Y's side and we all wince a communal wince. It is ending. I look to see that someone else is delivered of the check and make my way for the door, purposely disregarding years of anecdotes of violence befalling solo travelers. There are many roads to an ending. In fact, all roads bring you to the precipice. Is it bravery to insist (or is it stupidity?) that the hands steering the wheel be your own?

"Yes!" Wins

A man in the prime of his life feels himself balancing along the edge of becoming nearly sodden with despair over a series of failed relationships. He feels the old familiar smiling face cross his sagging cheeks and halfheartedly tosses himself into the indisputably cheerful and good natured Renovated City bar scene. He goes to the new waterfront bars named Lunacies and Crazy Ates and Players and in their well-lit, cavernous interiors he dances with self-conscious abandon to the guitar-heavy hits of yesterday made by screaming British youths. At the Sporting Scene he bungee jumps and slam dunks and even tosses himself at a wall of Velcro. In dapper suits of glistening Dacron he drinks microbrewed beers in dark brooding bottles. He says, "I work in NewLook Plaza," to young women in leopardskin tights and hair the size of the shrubs that surrounded his childhood home. He toys with the idea of a crew cut, leaving a little tail on the back, but fears deep in his soul that it would look ridiculous on a man his age. Maybe a speedboat to cruise the river. He goes to Gladstone's at the new Galorama Center and puts fluorescent clothing on his charge account and flirts with the salesgirl who tells him that this summer should be a real blowout. He has his doubts, but he allows the remark to cheer him and he drives home feeling glib and animated. He tunes in the Party Pig on the radio and hears the disc jockey ask the day's "Culture Question." And then he wonders, along with the rest of Renovated City, whether or not girls in bikinis should be allowed to sell hot dogs along the sides of roads and at sporting events. He toys with the idea of spending fifty cents when he gets home to call the number for "Yes." He has made up his mind on this. It is a good thing that women in bikinis sell hot dogs. It is in his mind a crucial issue that speaks to the heart of what America is all about.

At home he wonders if his civic concern in this area might actually move him into other areas of citizenship. Perhaps he will read up on this year's presidential candidates. Perhaps someday he himself will run for public office. His mind abuzz, he wonders what he believes in, what he feels strongly enough about to motivate him to run for public office. He likes the idea very much. He imagines his face on bumper stickers. He searches his mind for an issue, but the phone rings.

It is Amanda and she speaks to him in a quiet, seductive voice. He tries to remember who she is. One of the women from the bars, he is certain only of that. He gives out his number as a matter of course, always with the explanation that he has never done so before. Of course now he sees this as a trap he has laid for himself, one from which he cannot extricate himself without exposing himself as a liar. Amanda wants to meet for dinner. Her boyfriend, the one she told him all about, has left for good this time and she is glad; yes, she is certain of it: *this time* she is glad. She is delighted he has left and would like to get together because, she explains: 1) Time is short and, 2) things aren't at all like you think. "Things are never what you think." The fact that he has no idea what she means by this cryptic remark does not dissuade him from accepting when she names a certain restaurant in the Warehouse District renowned for its waterfront address, its faux-peeling paint, and its vaulted ceilings.

He showers and goes over and over in his mind the women he has met in this latest despair of his, the ones he approached with the secret hope, and belief, that the way to get over unhappiness in love is to compound it. Like the hair of the dog for a hangover, a broken heart is best mended with what caused it. He has been on the prowl for weeks and guesses, as he scrubs his body into a lather that feels especially cleansing for reasons he thinks he understands (new beginnings are like that), that he has given his number to perhaps thirty women, many of whom spoke of a boyfriend, although they were out alone or with girlfriends at night dressed in specifically enticing outfits and drinking specifically enticing beverages from long-stemmed glasses held in bony hands with painted nails.

There are messages being given out in most of what we do, he tells himself as he steps out of the shower, and the thought strikes him as sharp and insightful. He wonders, tentatively, if he really *is* as smart as he secretly thinks he is. The question makes him nervous though and he pulls on a pair of all-cotton flat-black bikini briefs and looks at himself in the mirror with some music going in the background. The Party Pig is now playing Journey, a band he remembers being popular just after he got out of college with his B.A. in marketing from a school immersed in a cornfield that at the time seemed to him to be the most thrilling place he'd ever been.

He turns himself to profile thinking he looks better from the side and then, seeing himself so exposed, he tries to imagine what it would be like selling hot dogs in a bikini. He tries to imagine what he himself would feel like standing out on the street wearing only these all-cotton flat-black briefs selling hot dogs to passing motorists. He imagines he would not do very much business at all and would in fact probably attract mostly jeers and humiliating catcalls and not much else. He knows vaguely the cruelty of which people are capable. Still, he tells himself, it is different for women who after all are much more naturally attractive and have a lifetime's experience being looked at in ways men cannot understand.

The disc jockey comes back on the radio after Journey, and says that "Yes" is winning by a resounding majority; by a majority of three-to-one, in fact, Renovated Citiers who listen to the Party Pig and are willing to spend fifty cents to have their opinions so tabulated, strongly believe women should be allowed to sell hot dogs in bikinis. He is gratified in knowing that he will not have to spend fifty cents to make sure "Yes" wins. The woman disc jockey encourages her sisters to chime in with their votes too. She does this playfully though, not as a feminist would, one of those awful makeupless bowwows you see on TV all the time trying to sound like everything would be fine if men were just castrated or whatever it is they want. Thinking the word "castration," just thinking it, makes him queasy as he imagines such a thing. He gets a chill and bends his naked knees together, cupping his sweaty palms together at his crotch. Fortunately his mind is once again wiped clean as a slate when, for the second time this evening, the phone rings. It is another woman; Alissa, and she says that she will be boating over the weekend out at the Islands. He does not know who this woman is, either, so coolly he wishes her well, saying it would be a fantastic weekend to join her out on the lake, if it only were not for his brother's children who were in need of supervision due to his brother's ruptured hernia, which he will be having removed or repaired or whatever it is they do to ruptured hernias. He feels the words spill from his tongue and is more than moderately pleased with his impromptu performance. He takes down Alissa's phone number and stuffs it in his underwear drawer.

He gets to the restaurant early thinking that will save him the embarrassment of not knowing what this woman looks like. She will find him seated already, a napkin over his slight paunch. He orders cappuccino from a young woman in tight black slacks whose rear end he happily admires in her retreat. It is a glorious world, he thinks. Then: too bad *she's* not wearing a bikini.

He looks through the menu, a giant booklet that makes him think of cartoons. He feels like a cartoon-small person looking through a normal-sized book. He laughs to himself believing randomly occurring flights of fancy such as these are what mark him as exceptionally intelligent and creative, the sort of person books are often written about. He adjusts his watch and lets out a delicate cough, letting the menu fall with a nearly imperceptible thud as the waitress returns with his black ceramic mug overflowing with cinnamon-topped cream perched on a tray of matching ceramic lined with brown cork. "Thank you," he says, leaning back into his chair, admiring the early dinner crowd of young Renovated Citiers here assembled. He feels a part of something—his generation perhaps—and breathes in deeply. He smokes leisurely, flicking his ashes in an unselfconscious bliss after every puff. He finishes both his cigarette and his cappuccino, and he is still alone.

He orders another cappuccino, fidgeting slightly, and he begins to reminisce, he saddles up his memory and goes on a carefree romp through the fecund pastures of sweet, sweet memories of his wild undergraduate days. He does so in a valiant effort to undermine the creeping suspicion that the woman, Amanda, will not show. He remembers wild fraternity parties where Ma, the old frat house chaperone, would get drunk and do crazy dances, rubbing her huge flabby breasts in mock ecstasy while they all cheered and guzzled beer after beer, certain that life would rarely deviate from the course they were already busily conjuring in their overexcited brains, if only they maintained diligence. Everything would go smoothly, forever and ever, because, well, because everything always had: and if it is not from the patterns of the past that we project the paths of the future, then from where?

Finally Amanda arrives in a flurry of packages and apologies saying there was a sale at Gladstone's at Twirling Towers she just couldn't get herself away from. The waitress returns in an instant and he holds his head up, knowing he will not be stood-up as this little-assed tart was obviously beginning to believe. Amanda orders a bloody mary and says *Oh, good, you smoke.*

She is okay, but *just* okay, although if he looks at her in a certain angle she is what can pass for pretty, but he is disappointed in how much he has to invest to get there. She says *You don't remember me* and he says *Oh, yes, certainly I do* trying to use big words and a dignified manner. But she corrects him and giggles and says *I'm sorry I'm not being fair and I think you might be angry but we've never met. You gave your card to a woman one night at Lunacies and she dropped it, by accident I'm sure. I picked it up. I probably wouldn't have called except two nights later I saw you give your card to a woman at Crazy Ates by the buffalo wing bar. So I figured you were, well, in the market.* She blushes and adds *And so am I.*

He is flattered and, he allows himself to admit, a little frightened. He thinks of popular movies of love gone sour, gone more than sour actually, sunk right down into the frightening world of dementia and he looks her over anew, this woman who has been following him, picking up other women's discarded phone numbers. What must be wrong with a person to drive her to such unseemly desperation?

They have dinner and talk mostly of Renovated City, comparing its grim, sooty-aired past with the happy, glistening atrium-filled present. They debate whether or not they would enjoy living in the new living-lofts down by the river. Neither is entirely convinced they would but they wholeheartedly concur in their admiration for the young artists that do, with their adventurous ways and their challenging, freethinking lifestyles.

He imagines he comes across as witty, light-spirited, and engaging. He listens in earnest to her long monologues, sipping delicately at his after-dinner coffee, which he takes black, thinking that the most sophisticated way to take after-dinner coffee. She tells him of her work as a promotional copywriter for a local university, speaking of it disinterestedly, but with what he perceives as an entirely admirable attempt to persuade him she feels otherwise. There follows an awkward silence, a wide, gaping cavity he has not the imagination nor the daring to fill. He watches in a slight panic as she then, miraculously it seems to him, summons from somewhere he guesses she visits regularly, a wellspring of vigor and enthusiasm and she shows him the stockings she bought at Gladstone's at Twirling Towers, producing them from the depths of one of her bags after a long search with a dramatic *Ta-da* that makes him think of magicians, and, incidentally, sends a half-empty glass of water reeling. *Oh, dear* she says and then laughs and he joins her. The waitress arrives with a rag and everyone agrees that they have lived through a funny, embarrassing event of the type this life brims with.

After coffee she excuses herself with a blush and he tries to summon admiration, or something approaching it, for her retreating rear end. Instead he thinks again of his college days and the tautness of the sorority girls' young bodies; the clean soft bodies they used to offer up to him shyly in the small room he had lit with a neon Budweiser sign. He remembers the self-confident banter he reeled off in a nearly forgotten effortlessness that he used to get them to that room. He remembers his glistening ways, the crispness of his collars and cuffs, even the full-fisted way he held a glass during dinner, peering over it, raised to his open mouth, smiling slyly.

When she returns she is polished over and combed anew. She looks away not wanting to draw attention to the work she has done to her face, yet wanting him to notice the results of it. She suggests a walk and he obliges. She takes his arm under hers, her packages in her free hand, and says *This is a lonely world* as they head toward the brand new stadium, where they can see a night game is being played. They hear muffled cheers as a policeman strolls past them twirling his nightstick expertly and whistling in pitch.

He thinks again of himself in his bikini briefs and wonders if before this night is over he will be so unattired for this woman's eyes. He is nearly certain that he will, and at the thought of it he pulls in his stomach and luxuriates in the puffing-out of his chest. He picks up the policeman's tune, although with considerably less expertise. He stuffs his hands in his pockets and listens to the sound of Amanda's shopping bags ruffling against each other. He has never been in love, he thinks. He never will be and there are a million reasons why. A million. Maybe one of them is that it doesn't exist. He doesn't know and he doesn't particularly want to think about it. He hears from the distance of the stadium the sound of bat on ball; a long ball for the home team by the sound of the crowd. He squeezes Amanda's arm and smiles into her eyes, wondering what goes on behind them, and if it's all that different than what goes on behind his own. He wonders why it is that he'll never know the answer to these questions, wonders why he thinks them at all. But now she is talking again, about something he can't quite concentrate on. He smiles though, as he thinks probably none of it matters, the thing to do is to just get through it all, looking, no *acting*, sharp.

Mouthfeel

Miles and Jenny started having problems about eighteen months into their marriage. The wedding had come during fairly hectic, exciting times for both of them. Miles had just finished his master's thesis—a joke, really—and had been hired on at the university as a composition instructor, enabling him to finally quit waiting tables at Johnny's. Jenny had just been promoted, too, to managing food technologist. This was a strange—but admittedly welcome—twist in her career. She had never planned on leaving lab work, but had found, to her absolute surprise, that she was gifted in the skills of effective management, and so with a combination of nostalgia and excitement she left the lab for a job up front. (All the guys on her polyol production team staged a symbolic lab-coat mothballing for her on her last day.) The promotion also meant a lot more money and the opportunity for even more vertical movement, which meant a lot to Jenny, who had put herself through graduate school on loans—the first woman in her family to get as much as a bachelor's degree, to say nothing of a master of science.

After a formal Catholic wedding (neither were religious, but Jenny's parents were paying the bills, after all), Miles and Jenny set about establishing a comfortable life for themselves. They rented a six-room apartment in an eighty-year-old building filled with other young professionals in the artsy section of town. The couple across the hall—there were only two apartments on a floor—were both architects and were very nice. Jenny especially liked them and she and Miles had them over for dinner twice in their first month, even though the apartment was hardly in a finished state. The first time, Jenny made a Thai dish she found in one of her new cookbooks and the next time Miles made his favorite meal, a mushroom-tofu-asparagus casserole with a giant Caesar salad.

The young couple thoroughly enjoyed what it looked like marriage was going to bring them—was already, in fact, bringing them. Miles felt, for the first time in his life, as he confessed late one night after a passionate session of mutually performed oral sex, a favorite of both of them (Jenny called it MPOing, as in, "Let's MPO," rather than the more traditional "69," which she found vulgar and lower class), that he finally *belonged*; that he was finally a *part* of something.

"All that angst in college," he said, Jenny cradled in his arms, freshly returned from brushing her teeth. "What was it for?"

"It's the professors," Jenny said. "They don't feel like they're doing their job unless they get you contemplating the abyss."

Miles thought about this for a minute; wondered if he expected his students to contemplate the abyss. "There's really not much to it," Miles said, tracing his finger along the curve of her spine, lingering near the bottom.

"The abyss?"

Miles nodded.

"No. It's overrated."

He snuggled closer to her, or tried: they were as close as two people could really get. "But now it all seems so simple. There *are* answers." Miles felt a chill run up his spine and the impulse, which he fought, to allow his eyes to water. His senses, all of them, seemed to be registering contentment after years and years of despair and bewilderment. Everything he could see, smell, feel, hear, even the taste in his mouth (he hadn't brushed); everything seemed full of wonder. "I don't know what I thought, really," he continued, the emotion evident in his cracking voice. "Everything's so obvious. But we resist."

Holding the naked body of his wife (his "wife"!) and feeling for the first time attached to the world of his fellow man, he glimpsed in a stunning, electric vision the great historic swell of humanity, growing and populating, building and destroying, procreating and dying, all throughout time; it revealed itself to him like a time-lapse film shot from space: a spinning blue sphere with a bustling, heroic race of beings shooting up out of the muck and shaping stones into cities and fears into religions. He was struck by the bravery and the wonder of it all, the utter improbability of any of it. The chaotic, random passage of eons leading (somehow, inevitably) to this moment; here in bed, holding his wife.

The same sorts of visions, he remembered, used to fill him with dread. The endlessness, the repetition of history, the blind allegiance to tradition: these all used to horrify him and, as a graduate student, offered evidence of the senselessness of existence, as he sat smugly in the back row of upper-level English courses, deconstructing culture with a smirk. But now he saw the comfort in the repetition, the beauty and warmth of tradition. He took a deep breath as his eyes watered. He was a part of something. Delicately, he parted Jenny's hair and kissed her gently on the top of her head. She was breathing now like she was asleep. Asleep in his arms, across his chest. His wife: Jenny.

Miles and Jenny were both very busy during this early period of their marriage, but they managed to devote a good portion of their energies toward decorating what they came to see as their overly large apartment. Since they didn't really want to spend too much time driving around, they did most of their shopping by phone and spent dozens of evenings and Saturdays thumbing through catalog after catalog, ordering chairs and bookshelves, candleholders and vases, wildly colored throw rugs and framed reproductions of the work of Edward Hopper (Miles' favorite) and Joan Miró (Jenny's). They got so accustomed to reciting their credit card numbers that they memorized them both. Jenny especially enjoyed a home furnishings store in Vermont called Pig Iron that took orders twenty-four hours a day. She would lie in their new cast iron bed at night, propped up on her pillows and thumb through their catalog, ordering bookends and picture frames. Miles' favorite place sold sleek black consumer electronics and frivolous high technology toys.

Soon, their large apartment was as filled as an apartment could reasonably be without drawing too much attention to itself. Jenny had wanted to order a bleached iron and driftwood bookshelf on which they could collect more items. ("Items" was the word they'd finally decided on one night in bed, thumbing through a catalog. Miles had started calling all their things tchotchkes, but Jenny bristled at this word, thinking of old ladies with blue hair. She didn't really have a suitable replacement, however, feeling that bric-a-brac was too provincial and *objet d'art* too pretentious. Miles then came up with items. "Let's call them items," he said. "We've decorated our apartment with 'various items.'" This seemed to please them both, so much so that they fell into a mad session of MPOing.)

After their second anniversary, things started to change when Jenny started bringing home dogs. Although Miles had never known this about her, apparently Jenny had a thing about stray dogs. After she brought the first one home—she told him that she had been suppressing the urge for years, but "just couldn't see the sense of it anymore"—she confessed that all through her childhood in suburban Chicago, she had driven her parents crazy bringing home all sorts of stray dogs—some, she admitted, that weren't really even strays, she said.

Miles' attention piqued at this comment and Jenny told him how, when she was fifteen, she was practicing tennis behind her high school, hitting a ball against a brick wall to work on her backhand, the one stroke, she said, that had kept her off the team.

"And as I was hitting, this very friendly dog came up. A mutt, and he wanted to play with the ball. I resisted him for a while, but he was just a puppy and was so full of that fun and love puppies have, that I stopped hitting and started throwing him the ball. I'd heave it as far as I could, and the little baby would just race after it, catch it, and bring it right back to me. He was just the most adorable thing. We played for the longest time, until dusk actually, and that's when I did it. I took his collar off and threw it down a sewer grate and took him home as a stray."

"It was someone's dog?" Miles said, astounded at this story.

"I know," she said, pouting playfully. "I've never told anyone before. Do you hate me?"

"Well," he said, "what happened?"

"We kept him. A year later we moved. He became the family dog. You met him, it's Willie."

Miles nodded. He thought of Willie's real family, an image of a crying little girl calling a name into the night came into his head.

"Didn't he die recently?"

"Yes, poor baby," she said dreamily. "He was fifteen."

Miles said an apartment was no place for a dog, and Jenny agreed and the first dog she brought home they only kept until Jenny found a home for her with someone at work. A few weeks later, she brought home another. Then another. She always found homes for the dogs, but sometimes there would be as many as four dogs in the apartment at one time. Often they fought with each other. Once Miles had had to hit one with a long pewter candlestick from Pig Iron to get it to let go of a small terrier that had wandered too close to its bowl during feeding.

After that incident, which left Miles feeling like a jailhouse guard, he and Jenny had a long, difficult fight that actually lasted something like a week. Miles had been feeling for some time that this dog thing was symptomatic of something severe, something real: like a mental disorder. He started thinking about daytime talk shows and Dear Abby columns, the great mass of people in this country who were baffled by uncontrollable impulses: to drink, to wash their hands, to cheat on their spouses. Maybe Jenny had one of these. He told her that the dog stuff was going to have to stop and practiced, when he was alone, bringing up this nagging notion of his that there was something wrong beyond the fact that it was irritating breaking up fights and stepping over (or on at least one case *in*) piles of excrement in the living room. Every time he tried to bring this subject up, however, Jenny would sidetrack him by arguing that what she was doing was morally comparable to the Danish family that hid Anne Frank in their attic. She said the distinction between human and animal life was "spurious at best." This always led the argument away from where Miles wanted to take it and into irresolvable, essentially theoretical discussions of moral relativity—while stray dogs yelped and chased each other around their very expensive furniture.

Miles finally gave up and retreated. He knew he would not win this battle. There was something very odd and unfamiliar in Jenny's eyes during these arguments. Something he didn't recognize, understand, or trust. Something, really, that he preferred not to see. He decided to wait it out.

And, after about a year of this intense interest in strays, Jenny slowly stopped bringing them home. Soon after the dog period, however, an even stranger and more severe trouble began. When it was all over, Miles often tried to pinpoint the exact beginning of the trouble, but he was never quite sure.

The first real incident occurred one night as the two lay in bed. Jenny was thumbing through a catalog of southwestern clothes looking for a new pair of espadrilles when she suddenly turned to Miles and said that she was disappointed in how little interest he showed in her dreams.

"Your dreams?" Miles asked, confused. "Like your dreams at night?"

"No, my *dreams*, Miles," she said, exasperated. "I have dreams, you know. You're not the only one in this house with dreams."

Miles was startled by the harshness in her voice. He turned to look at her and was stunned to see her face was red and her eyes squinted in intensity. He hadn't seen this look since the dog period—and even then, her eyes were more disoriented than angry. That night he saw a kind of rage, or panic, or some combination of the two.

"Do you even realize," she said, her voice strained, "that you're lying next to a *human being*?"

Miles reached out his arms to comfort her but she quickly pushed him away and turned on her side toward the wall. For the next hour she softly cried and then fell asleep. Miles was mortified. He barely moved all night. He remembered the terror he sometimes felt as a child in bed, convinced that there was a crazed murderer in the room and if he moved a muscle he would be violently killed. He'd trained himself to lay perfectly still for hours, in seeming peace, while his heart pounded. That night he may have drifted off a little toward dawn, but about this he couldn't be absolutely sure.

Several months later, Jenny's company had a picnic and softball game for the team of chemists and managers working on a fat-free replacer for cocoa butter in chocolate. This was the project Jenny had been working on for years, ever since getting out of graduate school. Every indication Miles had ever seen suggested that she enjoyed this work immensely, and she seemed to be fairly friendly with her coworkers, too. She often talked about her work with him at night. She'd say that food ingredient technology would become one of the most important fields on the planet as populations continued to increase. "I'm so thrilled to be a part of it," she'd say, impressing Miles with her sincerity.

He himself had no such lofty notions about his own role in the world. He felt that what he did with his time, teaching English composition at an urban campus and attempting to make it as a writer, was pointless, pure and simple. Teaching, he'd found, only sounded nice; his students were uninterested in what he had to say and many of them dressed like gangster rappers and actually frightened him. The only thing they ever showed any interest in was getting out of class. And writing, he had come to believe, was an act of pure ego. His desire to be published often made him feel like one of the clowns or Jesus freaks that hung out at football games or celebrity trials falling all over each other for a few seconds on television. As if being noticed, in itself, mattered in any real way.

Jenny played shortstop on the company softball team and during the game, Miles sat on the bleachers with a man he had seen at many of the other corporate outings sponsored by Jenny's company. His name was Sert, which was short for a very long Thai name, and he was the husband of one of the chief chemists. He always struck Miles as having a very Western personality, and this intrigued him. He dressed sloppily in old sweats and cursed frequently. He also spoke with a sarcastic inflection and snorted brief, completely unconvincing laughs at most everything he heard.

During the game, Sert and Miles joked about how poorly everyone on the teams played. Sert wore a T-shirt that read "Christ is Coming. (Look Busy.)" After the game was over, and Sert had had about three beers, he rose to greet his tiny wife—who played right field and dropped several routine fly balls—and said, "Scientists shouldn't bother with athletics. It's so fucking embarrassing."

After the game, there was a large barbecue and then Miles and Jenny went for a short walk in the woods surrounding the baseball diamond. Jenny had been pretty quiet and distant, and Miles was worried. She was walking ahead of him and eating an ice cream sandwich very deliberately, tonguing the ice cream out and leaving the wafers practically untouched. When she was finished with the ice cream, she took the wafers and threw them as far as she could into the woods and then fell to the ground with a thud.

Miles started to rush to her side, but she held up her hand to stop him.

"Do you know what we do—all those people out there? Do you know what we contribute to the world?"

Miles started to answer, but Jenny cut him off.

"Last week, I led a six-hour meeting that discussed—at length—the wording of a four-page brochure. We were in a room for six hours. A large black woman brought us lunch on a tray. It was assorted cold cuts. I was discussing the problems we were having encouraging our customers to believe an assertion we were making about mouthfeel. That's right, Miles, 'mouthfeel.'"

Jenny sat up and looked at Miles accusatorially. He sat down and lowered his eyes. He was wondering if there was anyone within hearing distance; what they would think if there was.

"Do you know how many times a week I say the word mouthfeel? Do you?"

"No," Miles admitted.

"Have you ever said the word mouthfeel?" Miles shook his head. "It's not a pleasant thing to say, mouthfeel. And do you know why? I'll tell you why: because it's not a word, that's why. You can't just go around making up words. Am I right?"

Miles said nothing but supposed that that was precisely how languages grew. And he actually kind of liked the word mouthfeel, liked the way it sounded in his head, repeating it over and over, as he sat there on a stump watching his wife's mind atrophy.

"There has to be a limit. The language has, I think, right now, *enough words*. There has to be a word or set of words—what are those called, phrases?—to describe the feeling of food in the mouth. Why we feel the need to just slap two words together and then to just go on like what we've done isn't a perversion, a crime, a holocaust!"

Miles again tried to protest, but Jenny just sat up and said, "Would you please just shut up, Miles? Please?"

"It's a waste of life. The earth just spins and spins," she went on, shaking her head, rolling it back and forth in the dirt. Miles noticed an old dead branch had gotten stuck in her ponytail. "So, anyway, I was leading this discussion—about *mouthfeel*—when this very dark, black woman who I had never seen before came in carrying this enormous tray of cold cuts. It was huge, the size of a good-sized kitchen table top, far larger than ours, anyway. And she moved with such grace and precision that she captivated my attention. Here is a woman, I thought, here is a *real* person, doing *real* work in the *real* world. She is setting out a tray of cold cuts. I envied her like you cannot believe, Miles. I wished to God I was a black servant woman."

Jenny was still lying on the ground. A long one or two minutes of absolute silence passed. "I am a foods scientist, Miles." Another pause. "I say the word mouthfeel dozens of times every week." Longer pause. "My car cost thirty-five thousand dollars." She went on, and on. "I spent seven years earning a bachelor's and then a master's degree." "Once, I spent eighty dollars on a tennis racket and put it in my closet and never used it. Ever." "Because I wanted to, I once stole a stray."

Miles sat in dumb wonder, wondering who he should tell that Jenny was going insane, where he should go. He remembered visiting New York when he was twenty-two to see a friend of his who grew up in Manhattan. On the last day of the trip, his friend said he wanted to show Miles the funniest, scariest thing in Manhattan. They took the A train up into Harlem somewhere, the Harlem you see on documentaries. His friend said it really wasn't that dangerous, especially during the day, and to just act aloof. (Aloof was this particular friend's favorite word and he often told Miles that the key to successful living was to act aloof no matter what happens.) Finally they got to a rear entrance of Harlem Hospital and Miles' friend led him to a dented sign on the street that read, "24-Hour Walk-In Psychiatric Emergency." "That," his friend told him that day, pointing at the sign, "is the perfect metaphor for New York."

"All roads lead to Rome," Jenny continued. "This is a memo: Subject: Mouthfeel." "My mother never knew peace."

Finally Jenny stopped and stood up, looked around with a wild look in her eyes and then peeled off her pants. "Let's MPO!" she said, nearly shouting.

Miles was stunned and must have looked it because Jenny started laughing devilishly as she struggled to make her way over to him with her pants around her knees. She fell and then started crawling across the forest floor. "Come on," she said, "I want that tongue of yours surfing between my legs."

Miles looked back over his shoulder just as Jenny grabbed his belt and started undoing it. He tried to push her away but was torn between the impulse to run and the impulse to help her: somehow.

Jenny undid his zipper and had her hand in there as she struggled to simultaneously remove her shirt. Finally, Miles leapt up and pushed Jenny away from him. She fell down on her back, her pants at her heels and her shirt half off. Lying there, her hands flew up to her face and she started crying; sobbing at first but this soon led to hyperventilating and wailing. Miles jumped to her side and held her as he pulled her clothes back on. He rocked her head in his arms. He pulled the leaves and twigs from her hair. He said, "Shhh," over and over again. He tried to hide the fact that his own heart was racing. He looked around at the thick woods and thought of them as being filled with hostile food technologists, gathered together out there somewhere, in a clearing by a badly kept baseball diamond, drinking beer and chatting amiably. He pictured Sert and his tiny wife, imagining how different—how normal—their married lives probably were.

After a few minutes of rocking and petting, Jenny started coming around and soon was able to pull herself together enough to get past her coworkers and into the car. On the ride home Jenny wept quietly, her face pressed against the passenger window. Miles nearly had to carry her up the two flights of stairs to their apartment. He gently put her to bed and made her a cup of warm milk. When he brought it to her, he put on a Keith Jarret solo piano CD and got into bed with her. He sat above the covers, fully clothed, and patted her head as she sipped the milk. Each time the CD ended he picked up the remote and started it over from the beginning. Jenny finally fell asleep around eight in the evening and slept until five o'clock the next afternoon. Neither one ever mentioned the incident in the woods again.

Things then settled down for a while, and Miles convinced himself that Jenny was just going through a difficult time and that it would all pass. He suspected, nonetheless, that he should probably tell someone about what was going on, but every time he tried, he felt foolish and somehow guilty. If he went to someone, now, would they chastise him for waiting so long? Wasn't it perfectly obvious that there was something wrong and hadn't it been for some time? So, why had he waited?

At the end of their second summer together, Miles was picked up for another year at the university and there was chance for a better paying, slightly more permanent position at a community college the year after that. Jenny suggested that they take a vacation in September before the school year started, and they called a travel agent to make arrangements. Miles wanted to go to North Carolina, but they decided on Nova Scotia because Jenny said she hated the heat and couldn't bear the idea of lying on a beach all day in some tropical hellhole.

"North Carolina is hardly a tropical hellhole," Miles said before giving in.

"Jesus Fucking Christ, Miles. Could you please not savage me with sarcasm every time your vision and mine clash? I am human, you know. There is a heart in here that beats and has feelings and everything. I'm not a plant or a painting hanging on a wall." Miles' heart raced as she spoke. He saw it starting again.

Nova Scotia was just as Miles imagined it: rocky beaches, brisk air, colorfully painted but badly fading houses and boats. He and Jenny rented a three-room cabin near a bay in a town of professional fishermen and almost no tourists. This was as Jenny said she wanted it. She said that she "absolutely couldn't endure the thought of fighting a lot of moronic tourists for a quaint moment."

"I wish I could just be," she said their first night in bed in the cabin. They had sex (a fantastic MPO) for the first time in weeks, and Miles was feeling at ease. "Why is it so hard to just be?"

One day that week, as they were hiking, Miles noticed that Jenny's walk had changed. They were hiking on an old trail that a fisherman named Claude had told them went to a small quarry where there were lots of Indian relics. ("Maybe," Jenny said in a tone that seemed to Miles to be both sarcastic and sincere at the same time, "Indian relics will bring meaning to our lives.") As they were hiking, Miles noticed that Jenny was casting her weight forward with a great eagerness and determination. She also seemed to be thrusting her hips back and forth, almost comically. At first, he thought it was just that they were hiking, that it was the weight of her pack (which really wasn't that much), or the incline of the land (again: not that much).

When they got to the quarry, though, Jenny tossed her pack aside. They were no longer "hiking," and the strange new walk remained. They spent about an hour digging around in slate for Indian relics, but they found nothing. Just as they were about to give up, though, Jenny picked something up and squealed in delight. Miles looked over at her as she started jumping up and down, yelling, "It's an arrowhead, Miles, it's an arrowhead!" Miles rushed over, but when he got there, all it looked like to him was an ordinary piece of slate, like thousands he'd been tossing aside all day long. He was afraid to say anything, though, and tried his best to be excited.

"Just think," she said, "we're the first people to touch this in maybe a thousand years."

That night Jenny went into town for food and came back with two cans of tuna, tuna helper, and a badly stained casserole dish, which she said she bought at a flea market. "I don't know what came over me," she said. "I was wondering what I felt like eating, and I just had this very warm flashback to when I was a kid and my mother would make us all tuna casseroles, you know?"

Miles didn't know. His mother was an elitist when it came to food. She almost certainly would have cut her throat before allowing her children to eat tuna casserole.

"I mean, my God, think about it Miles: *casseroles*." Jenny's body actually quivered at the word. Her knees literally dipped. "If you distill us down to our essence, this is what we are," she said as she held up the box of tuna helper. "We *are* tuna helper, Miles. That is what we *are*."

After dinner, Jenny and Miles had tremendous sex on the floor beside the kitchen table. Miles was shocked at some of the things Jenny did and, more so, at the things she said. They reminded him, in fact, of the incident in the woods. When he pulled out of her at the end, she smeared his stuff all over her belly and up onto one of her breasts. She then squeezed the breast and pulled it up to her mouth and licked it clean, something she had never, ever done. Something Miles had never seen done in real life. As far as he knew, only porno actresses did it.

He forced what he hoped would look like a decadent smile across his face and then collapsed on top of her.

Later that night in bed, Jenny was glum and distant. She was trying to read a book written by an eminent entomologist recounting his unlikely ascent to the top of his unlikely profession, but it seemed to bore her. She turned over a lot, continually adjusted her T-shirt, and kept reading back over pages she had already read.

Finally she flung the book onto the bed and stared at it like it had appeared in her hands from nowhere, like its connections to her—the fact that she had gone to a store specifically to buy it after reading a review; that she had packed it into a suitcase after expressing concerns that maybe she should bring something lighter—were gone, had never in fact existed.

"This guy," she said, her arms folded across her chest and nodding with utter contempt toward the book, "is like the *biggest* asshole, I think . . . yes, the biggest *asshole* alive on the earth today."

"What about Newt Gingrich?" Miles asked.

She looked at him cross-eyed, her head cocked and pulled back. "Are you making fun of me?" she asked. "Was that some kind of joke?"

Miles tried to endure the glare of her eyes, just to prove to himself that he could, but he finally gave up and lowered his head in what felt to him like humiliation.

She then turned the light off and flung herself onto her pillow. Miles heard her mutter, "asshole," and tried to tell himself that she was talking about the entomologist.

On their last night, Jenny started packing some things together. When she got to the casserole dish, she held it up and stared quizzically at it for a second before shrugging her shoulders and tossing it in the garbage. She had everything packed and ready to go well before nine o'clock. Miles was reading the entomologist's book to see what had prompted Jenny's declaration about him. Everything he'd read about the man seemed to suggest he was eminently likable, wise, and decent, and that was just as Miles found him.

Jenny was growing restless, though, and Miles was having a hard time focusing on the book. He tossed it aside and asked her what she was doing, what she was looking for.

"The arrowhead," she said. "I can't find the arrowhead."

"I haven't seen it in a couple of days," Miles said. "Are you sure you didn't pack it?"

She stared at Miles and shook her head, as though he were becoming impossible to bear. "I'm not even sure I exist," she muttered and continued scanning the cabin. "For all I know, I'm an experiment in a petri dish in a lab spinning on a planet in a gaseous cluster of . . . gaseous things . . . eight trillion light-years from here and nine billion years before any of us were born."

Jenny's voice got lower and lower as her search became more

and more frantic. Finally, she eyed the luggage and started throwing it open, tossing their clothes in giant, dramatic arcs across the room. Miles had never seen anything like it and when his favorite sweater landed in the sink, along with the residue of dinner (a cheese, broccoli, and Ritz cracker casserole) he flew into a rage.

"Hey!" he yelled. "That's my sweater."

"Oh, get over it, you fag," she snapped. "I'm looking for something important here."

"Oh, for God's sake," Miles said, dashing to the sink and retrieving his sweater. "That was no arrowhead. It was a triangular piece of slate. There were no tooling marks on it, the edges weren't shaped. All I know about arrowheads is what I remember from Boy Scouts, and even I know that was no arrowhead."

Miles realized the fury consuming him had been building for a long time. He stared down at the greasy mess in the sink and the stain it had left on his favorite sweater. Everything he had been telling himself for months about how he was going to deal with the fact that his wife was clearly losing touch with reality was gone. He could remember none of it. Or rather, he could remember it, but it all seemed so useless, so banal, so weak. "I think there's something *seriously* wrong with you," he nearly shouted. "I think something's happened to you."

Jenny paused for a second to consider this. She froze in place and looked off into the distance. And then she did the last thing in the world Miles ever expected: she attacked him. Screaming ferociously, like a Hollywood Indian on the warpath, she lunged at him, throwing herself an incredible distance through the air and hitting him, knees first, in his chest. The force knocked him down and his head spun in confused panic. Still screaming, Jenny lifted her arm to smack her husband across the face, but Miles had regained at least the composure to reach up and grab her arm. Once he had that in hand he felt fairly confident, despite the screaming and her frantic twitching, that he could contain her. He was almost a foot bigger and eighty pounds heavier than her. He held her until she stopped squirming and then stood up with her and let her go.

Unfortunately, though, she was only playing dead, because after catching her breath she looked back up at him, again with the look of a wild animal in her eyes, and jumped back into action. She grabbed an empty wine bottle over by the kitchen and smashed it in half on the counter. She held it by the throat, looked up at him and said, in a B-movie diabolical voice, "I'm going to cut your fucking head off."

Having handled her so easily before, Miles was not so scared this time, despite the weapon. He let her chase him around the cabin a bit, but, ultimately, he had no choice but to call the police after putting a move on her, kicking the bottle out of her hands and tackling her. His first thought was that he would just lay there on top of her until she calmed down, but after several minutes that began to seem unlikely. Although she was not that strong, she was not giving up and after a few minutes it was a strain to keep her subdued.

"I'm going to have to call the police," he told her.

She only screamed and tried to get away. He got her in a scissors lock and dragged her over to the phone, where he discovered that 911 is meaningless in Canada. He finally got an operator and told her that he needed the police and an ambulance right away. He had to constrain her for a full twenty minutes until they came. Miles expected to be ridiculed, but to his surprise was not. The paramedics restrained Jenny on a stretcher and stuck a needle in her arm as the police sat with Miles and very calmly listened to his story.

When he got to the part about the arrowhead, the younger officer stopped him and said it was a federal crime in Canada to remove indigenous peoples' artifacts from the country.

The doctor at the Bursting Valley Medical Clinic told Miles that there really wasn't anything "long term" he could do for her, since she was an American.

"I pity you folks down there, if it's worth anything," he said. "With your Newt Gingriches and your insurance cartels." He said that in a gesture of solidarity and pity, he would allow her to spend the night. "I can lose the paperwork for thirty hours or so, but then she'll have to leave."

He was able to patch up Miles' three or four cuts and scrapes.

He even gave Miles a brochure produced by the Canadian Ministry of Mental Health on the subject of spousal abuse. "We have to give it to everyone who's been hit by a spouse," he told him and shrugged. As he was leaving Miles thanked him for looking the other way about the citizenship thing, and the doctor nodded and patted Miles on the shoulder.

"I'm an escaped American," he said. "I came rather than firebomb a jungle. I know what it's like down there."

Miles said nothing. He wasn't even sure he knew what he meant or if this young man was even old enough to have avoided the Vietnam draft.

"Take care of yourself," he said, "and get her back across the border and into a hospital soon."

That night Miles spent alone in the cabin by the bay. It was starting to get cool and he had a fire going as he cleaned up, his sweater soaking in the bathroom sink. After dark he sat by the phone practicing the phone call he would make to Jenny's mother, explaining everything, about how little things had been accumulating over the last year or two and that it was pretty clear now that something was wrong.

He poured himself a drink before making the call and then was relieved to get Jenny's father instead. He thought that, as a man, he would be less likely to become overly emotional; and he was right. He listened calmly to the whole story (Miles began with the stray-dog collecting), expressing shock in manageable doses, and then cordially thanked Miles for letting them know. He suggested that when they got back some sort of psychiatric care would be in order and volunteered to begin asking around. Miles said that would be a good idea and then, as they were about to hang up, Jenny's father said, "Oh, Miles, one other thing just for the record, not that it really matters one way or another, but, Willie was not a stray. Jenny's mother and I paid four hundred dollars for that dog from a breeder out in Missing County."

When he hung up the phone, Miles thought about Jenny's parents, two seemingly normal, happy, well-adjusted people. He thought of his own parents. The architects that he and Jenny lived next to. All the thousands—millions—of people he'd seen in his life. Either what was happening to Jenny was a one-in-a-million accident of fate or genes, or this happened all the time but nobody talked about it. Miles thought it was probably the second, probably this happened all the time: people just went nuts, stopped acting like people act, started despising the idiocy of their work, the emptiness of their apartments, the solitude of the mind. It really was too much to stand. The work, the highways, the rewards. None of it matched up, nothing led to anything. There was no line to follow, no continuity.

In the morning, Miles had to talk to the owners of the cabin about the damages Jenny had done. They were fairly helpful, as he'd come to learn Canadians generally were, and when he got everything together, he took a cab to the medical center, where he found Jenny in a private room.

She smiled up at him and blushed, covered to her chin in a light blue sheet. "I'm crazy," she said. "I've gone bonkers, Miles."

Miles said nothing and tried to smile.

The Iowa Short Fiction Award and John Simmons Short Fiction Award Winners

1997
Thank You for Being Concerned and Sensitive, Jim Henry
Judge: Ann Beattie

1997
Within the Lighted City,
Lisa Lenzo
Judge: Ann Beattie

1996
Hints of His Mortality,
David Borofka
Judge: Oscar Hijuelos

1996
Western Electric, Don Zancanella
Judge: Oscar Hijuelos

1995
Listening to Mozart,
Charles Wyatt
Judge: Ethan Canin

1995
May You Live in Interesting Times, Tereze Glück
Judge: Ethan Canin

1994
The Good Doctor,
Susan Onthank Mates
Judge: Joy Williams

1994
Igloo among Palms,
Rod Val Moore
Judge: Joy Williams

1993
Happiness, Ann Harleman
Judge: Francine Prose

1993
Macauley's Thumb,
Lex Williford
Judge: Francine Prose

1993
Where Love Leaves Us,
Renée Manfredi
Judge: Francine Prose

1992
My Body to You,
Elizabeth Searle
Judge: James Salter

1992
Imaginary Men, Enid Shomer
Judge: James Salter

1991
The Ant Generator,
Elizabeth Harris
Judge: Marilynne Robinson

1991
Traps, Sondra Spatt Olsen
Judge: Marilynne Robinson

1990
A Hole in the Language,
Marly Swick
Judge: Jayne Anne Phillips

1989
Lent: The Slow Fast,
Starkey Flythe, Jr.
Judge: Gail Godwin

1989
Line of Fall, Miles Wilson
Judge: Gail Godwin

1988
The Long White,
Sharon Dilworth
Judge: Robert Stone

1988
The Venus Tree,
Michael Pritchett
Judge: Robert Stone

1987
Fruit of the Month, Abby Frucht
Judge: Alison Lurie

1987
Star Game, Lucia Nevai
Judge: Alison Lurie

1986
Eminent Domain, Dan O'Brien
Judge: Iowa Writers' Workshop

1986
Resurrectionists,
Russell Working
Judge: Tobias Wolff

1985
Dancing in the Movies,
Robert Boswell
Judge: Tim O'Brien

1984
Old Wives' Tales,
Susan M. Dodd
Judge: Frederick Busch

1983
Heart Failure, Ivy Goodman
Judge: Alice Adams

1982
Shiny Objects, Dianne Benedict
Judge: Raymond Carver

1981
The Phototropic Woman,
Annabel Thomas
Judge: Doris Grumbach

1980
Impossible Appetites,
James Fetler
Judge: Francine du Plessix Gray

1979
Fly Away Home, Mary Hedin
Judge: John Gardner

1978
A Nest of Hooks, Lon Otto
Judge: Stanley Elkin

1977
The Women in the Mirror,
Pat Carr
Judge: Leonard Michaels

1976
The Black Velvet Girl,
C. E. Poverman
Judge: Donald Barthelme

1975
Harry Belten and the Mendelssohn Violin Concerto,
Barry Targan
Judge: George P. Garrett

1974
After the First Death There Is No Other, Natalie L. M. Petesch
Judge: William H. Gass

1973
The Itinerary of Beggars,
H. E. Francis
Judge: John Hawkes

1972
The Burning and Other Stories,
Jack Cady
Judge: Joyce Carol Oates

1971
Old Morals, Small Continents,
Darker Times,
Philip F. O'Connor
Judge: George P. Elliott

1970
The Beach Umbrella,
Cyrus Colter
Judges: Vance Bourjaily and
Kurt Vonnegut, Jr.